Here's Where I Stand

JanayJourney

Table of contents

Copyright Page
Disclaimer
Dedication
Chapter 1 – Here in the Dark
Chapter 2 – I Come Before You
Chapter 3 – You Took My Shame
Chapter 4 – So Much to Give
Chapter 5 – Praying You'll Stay
Chapter 6 – Lord, Please Hear Me
Chapter 7 – Who I Am
Chapter 8 – Save Me, Don't Let Me Stray
Chapter 9 – You Said I Had to Change
Chapter 10 – My Soul's Not Dying
Chapter 11 – In You I'm Stronger
Chapter 12 – Through the Fire
Chapter 13 – Don't Let Go of My Hand
Chapter 14 – I Walk by Faith
Chapter 15 – I Understand
Chapter 16 – We Walk So Far
Chapter 17 – You Show Us Who We Are
Chapter 18 – Let Your Love Light the Way
Chapter 19 – Boldly Say
Chapter 20 – Stand Tall
Chapter 21 – I Am Counted
Chapter 22 – I'm Counting on You
Chapter 23 – With Your Grace
Chapter 24 – Love Me, Use Me
Chapter 25 – Lead Me Too
Chapter 26 – And I'll Make It Through
Chapter 27 – Jesus, I'm Counting on You
Chapter 28 – In You I See
Chapter 29 – Here's Where I Stand (Reprise)
Chapter 30 – This Is Who I Am
Chapter 31 – I Am Yours
Chapter 32 – Here's Who We Are
Chapter 33 – Grace Carried Me
Chapter 35 – I'll Make It Through
Epilogue – Standing Together
Author's Note
Reader Reflection & Discussion Guide
Reader Reflection & Prayer Guide
About the Author

Copyright Page

Disclaimer

This book is a work of fiction, inspired by themes of faith, redemption, and surrender. While the story draws on spiritual truths and biblical references, the characters, events, and settings are products of the author's imagination. Any resemblance to real persons, living or dead, or actual events is purely coincidental.

The content within this book is not intended to serve as professional counseling, therapy, or pastoral advice. Readers facing personal struggles are encouraged to seek guidance through prayer, trusted mentors, licensed professionals, or faith leaders in their local community.

All Scripture references are included for inspirational purposes. The author makes no claim of theological authority beyond creative storytelling rooted in faith.

By reading this book, you acknowledge that the story is designed to encourage, uplift, and inspire—not to replace personal spiritual growth or professional support.

Dedication

To the One who found me in the dark,
   held me when I was broken,
   and loved me back to life—
   Jesus, this story belongs to You.

   To every reader carrying shame,
   wrestling with faith,
   or wondering if God can still use you—
   may these pages remind you:
   His grace is enough.

   And to my three beautiful children,
   my greatest blessings and my daily reminder of hope—
   this book is for you.

Chapter 1 – Here in the Dark

The wind rattled the edges of the old church window like it was trying to shake heaven awake. Eva Hart sat hunched in the back pew, shoulders curled in, hands trembling as they gripped a worn leather-bound journal. The only light in the sanctuary came from a single flickering votive, its flame casting long, uncertain shadows against the altar.

It had been three years since she'd stood there.

Three years since her voice had filled this place with praise.

Three years since her hands, once raised in joyful surrender, had fallen—along with everything else.

The stage lights used to warm her face like sunlight. Now, the world only offered cold headlines, colder whispers. Her name had once been printed on conference banners, worship setlists, and devotionals. But one messy heartbreak—one public unraveling—and all of it disappeared like fog in the morning sun.

A scandal. A mistake. A betrayal she never saw coming.

Eva didn't know what hurt more: what he did, or the silence from those she had trusted most.

Her fingers slowly turned to a blank page. The ink of the pen bled softly into the paper as she began to write—not like a leader, not like a songwriter or speaker, but like a woman completely undone.

Here I am again, God. I don't even know if You're still listening. But I'm here. In the dark. Just me and You. That has to count for something, right?

She paused. Her breath shuddered.

You know who I used to be. Maybe everyone else forgot, but You saw it. You were there. You were the One I sang to. You were the One who held me when the stage lights faded and the real world came rushing in like a flood.

So if You're still there—if You haven't turned Your face from me too—then please... please speak. Because I'm tired of this silence. I'm tired of being invisible.

She wiped her eyes with the sleeve of her hoodie, then closed the journal slowly and pressed it against her chest. For a long while, she just breathed. In and out. In and out. The kind of breath you learn to take when tears are the only prayer you have left.

From the shadows above the stage, a familiar shape stirred.

The cross.

Not ornate. Not backlit. Just wood. Simple. Worn.

But tonight, it pierced her like light through fog.

Eva stood slowly and walked to the altar. The echo of her boots on the stone floor reminded her she was real—still here. Still alive, though she hadn't felt alive in a long time.

"I miss You," she whispered aloud.

The words sounded foreign. Small.

"I miss being close to You. I miss waking up knowing I'm in Your will, not just... surviving."

She knelt. Not out of obligation, but out of something older, deeper. That instinct that pulled a child toward her Father when she's scraped her knees and can't stop bleeding.

The tears came quietly this time. Not as a flood—but like a slow, steady rain softening the soil of her soul.

"I know what they say. That I ruined my ministry. That I shouldn't have let it get that far with him. That I lost the right to lead, to sing, to speak..."

Her voice cracked.

"But what about You, God? What do You say?"

She waited in silence. Seconds passed. Then minutes. The creaks of the church shifted like whispers, like time folding in.

No booming voice from the sky.

No angel in white robes.

Just a memory. A melody.

Faint, but familiar.

It was a line from a worship song she wrote when she was nineteen. Back before the platforms and the labels. Back when worship was messy and honest and barefoot in her bedroom.

"Here in the dark, I come before You…"

She opened her mouth before she even realized she was singing.

"Jesus, I lift up my hands…"

Her voice was cracked and raw, like an old vinyl left in the sun—but it was hers. And for the first time in a long time, she wasn't performing. She was pleading.

She finished the verse with a whisper:

"To honor Your name… You took my shame… You took my pain…"

The last note hung in the air like a held breath.

Then, silence again.

But this time, it wasn't empty. It felt… sacred.

Eva stood. Slowly. Carefully. The journal still pressed to her chest, now warm from where her hands had clung to it. She traced a finger along the edge of the altar.

"I'm not asking for the spotlight," she whispered, her voice steadier now. "I'm not even asking to lead again. I just… I want to feel like Yours. I want to come home."

As she turned to leave, she heard it again—not in the air, but in her spirit. A single line, gentle and firm, unmistakably Him:

"You never stopped being Mine."

She stopped mid-step. Closed her eyes.

That voice—oh, she knew it. No stage, no crowd, no title had ever filled her the way that voice did.

Eva exhaled, deeply this time. A full breath. For the first time in forever, she felt her soul unclench.

It would be a long road. She knew that. Healing wasn't a single night in an old church. It was day after day of choosing truth over lies, presence over performance.

But tonight… tonight was a start.

She stepped out into the early dawn. The wind was colder now, but it no longer bit. She pulled her shawl closer and walked toward her car, heart pounding, feet steady.

Tomorrow, she would start small.

Maybe a phone call to her old friend Mia.

Maybe a visit to the women's shelter down the block.

Maybe just a worship song in her kitchen while making coffee.

But tonight—here in the dark—Eva stood.

Not as the girl with the perfect voice.

Not as the woman who lost everything.

But as a daughter, coming home.

Chapter 2 – I Come Before You

Eva stood outside the weathered brick building, hands deep in the pockets of her coat, as if she could hide from the weight pressing on her chest. The wind tugged at the ends of her scarf, the morning air brisk with the scent of leaves, old wood, and something else—memory.

The white cross above the steeple had chipped since she'd last seen it. But it still stood tall. Still pointed heavenward.

Just like she used to.

A small group of congregants filtered through the front doors, warm greetings spilling out alongside them. Families. Older couples. Young kids skipping ahead of their parents. All familiar. All distant. Eva stayed still, hoping not to be noticed.

She hadn't come to be seen.

She came because her spirit needed it—craved it like water after wandering a desert. And she knew —deep down—if she didn't return here now, she might never return at all.

A deep breath. One step. Then another.

She slipped inside quietly, her boots hushed against the sanctuary's carpeted aisle. The interior hadn't changed. The same soft blue walls. The same wooden pews with the faded hymnals in the slots. Even the same dusty sunlight spilling through the high stained-glass windows.

She walked past rows of people smiling, chatting, and leafing through bulletins, then eased into the very back pew, her body folding in on itself like she might disappear completely.

She wasn't sure she deserved to be here.

Not after everything.

Her fingers curled around the edge of the pew, knuckles white. The worship band began to play a familiar intro—soft guitar, the swelling of keys. The congregation stood, voices lifting like incense, and Eva remained seated.

The lyrics cut deep:

"Come just as you are, come and see…"

She stared straight ahead, willing herself not to cry.

Just as you are, she thought bitterly. Do they really mean that? Would they still say it if they knew what I did? What I lost?

The song continued, but Eva wasn't singing. Not yet. She was too busy remembering.

The last time she'd stood on that very stage—two and a half years ago—she had no idea it would be her final time leading worship here. She had poured out her heart in that service. Smiled through the pain of a dissolving relationship. Said nothing as rumors circled, as whispers chased her down hallways and parking lots.

The truth had never really mattered in the end. The optics won.

She closed her eyes.

"Lord, why did You let me fall so far?"

The shame clung to her like a second skin. She'd repented. Over and over. Cried until her soul felt wrung dry. But healing wasn't neat. And grace? Grace was sometimes hardest to receive when you thought you had to earn your way back into God's presence.

The pastor took the stage—Pastor Miriam. Eva hadn't known she would be preaching today. Miriam had always seen her, even when others turned away. She'd tried reaching out in the early months, but Eva ignored the calls. She was afraid of pity, of kindness. Sometimes it felt easier to nurse your wounds than accept someone trying to help you stand.

But something in Pastor Miriam's voice today felt different. It wasn't just a sermon. It was a message—a personal one.

"Some of you feel like you've disqualified yourselves from God's love. Like you've messed up so badly, there's no coming back. But I came to tell you this morning—He never changed His mind about you. His calling is still alive. His grace didn't expire. And He's not just waiting for you to be perfect. He's waiting for you to be willing."

Eva blinked fast. Her throat thickened.

Pastor Miriam looked right to the back. Right at her.

Not through her.

At her.

The words pierced through the fog of shame like a pinprick of light.

Eva glanced up toward the stage—toward the empty mic stand she once clung to like a lifeline. Her mind flooded with moments. Mornings rehearsing before anyone arrived. Prayer circles backstage. The first time she sang her own song to a packed congregation and felt the Spirit descend like holy fire.

She remembered how alive she felt in His presence. How she never had to strive to be enough—she was enough, because He called her.

Tears welled behind her eyes again, but this time… not from guilt.

From grief.

Grief for the years she'd lost. For the lies she believed. For the voice inside her that still told her she didn't belong.

"Jesus," she whispered. "I don't know if I can be that girl again. But I miss You. I miss that closeness."

The worship team began the final song.

"I lift up my hands to honor Your name…"

Eva's heart clenched.

That was her lyric. Her song.

She'd written it years ago, during a midnight prayer in her dorm room, tears soaking the pages of her notebook as she cried out to God for purpose. It had become the song of the youth ministry. The anthem of her calling.

And now they were singing it without her.

She should have felt jealous. Replaced.

But instead…

She felt seen.

Because the song wasn't about her. It never was. It was about Him. It had always been.

Eva rose slowly to her feet, her hands trembling. For a long moment, she stood still. Watching. Listening.

Then she lifted her hands—just slightly. Not high. Not performative. But real.

Jesus, I come before You.

No mic.

No spotlight.

No audience.

Just surrender.

Something inside her cracked. The hard shell of bitterness, of self-preservation—something holy broke through. The tears came freely now. The music surrounded her, but it wasn't loud. It was tender. A balm.

"You took my shame… You took my pain…"

Eva whispered it like a promise.

And this time, she believed it.

When the service ended, she stayed behind. Let the crowd filter out. Let the chatter fade.

She walked to the altar, not because she had to—but because she wanted to.

Pastor Miriam was there, stacking her notes, soft and unhurried.

Eva hesitated.

Then spoke.

"Hi."

Miriam turned.

And smiled.

"Eva," she said. No judgment. No surprise. Just warmth.

"I wasn't sure if I should come," Eva said quickly, fumbling with the edges of her sleeve. "I just… I don't know what I'm doing anymore."

Miriam stepped closer. "You came. That's enough for today."

Eva's chin trembled. "Do you really think God still… wants me?"

Miriam didn't answer with words.

She pulled her into a hug.

And in that embrace, Eva felt something she hadn't felt in years.

Belonging.

Not to a place.

Not to a role.

But to God.

She didn't know what tomorrow would hold.

But today—here in this sacred, familiar space—Eva came before Him.

And He met her there.

Chapter 3 – You Took My Shame

The sound of the washer hummed softly in the background, the only noise filling Eva's small apartment. She sat cross-legged on the living room rug, a mug of lukewarm tea in one hand and her journal open beside her. Sunlight poured through the blinds in angled slices, catching the dust in the air like floating particles of memory.

She hadn't intended to revisit the past today. But healing rarely asks for permission. It arrives like a whisper, unexpected and firm: It's time.

She reached for the shoebox tucked under the couch—the one she hadn't opened in nearly two years. Inside were folded letters, photos, a dried corsage from a gala, and a ring.

The ring.

Simple. Silver. No stone. Just a tiny engraved cross on the inner band.

Her breath caught.

It had been his idea—a "purity promise" turned engagement turned… disaster.

She touched the cold metal, her fingers remembering how it once felt warm from his hand. Then, carefully, she laid the ring on the journal like a confession.

And the memories came rushing back.

Two years earlier.

The announcement had gone live on the church's Instagram page:

"We are so excited to celebrate the engagement of our worship director, Eva Hart, and our youth pastor, Noah Wilder!"

The photo had been sweet. Smiling. Eva's head tilted against his shoulder, her hand resting over his heart. She had never looked more radiant. Or so people said.

She'd thought it was real.

He said all the right things: that she was his answered prayer, that they would build a ministry together, that she made him better.

But things had started to change within a few months.

It began with small things: canceled date nights for "urgent meetings," phone calls Eva wasn't supposed to overhear, flirtatious comments from young women in the youth ministry brushed off as "jokes."

She asked questions.

He offered gaslighted reassurance.

When she found a series of texts—too intimate, too flirtatious to be innocent—he swore it meant nothing.

And she believed him.

Because she loved him.

Because she was terrified that if it wasn't him, it might not be anyone.

But the truth couldn't stay buried.

One night, after a worship practice, she returned to the church office to retrieve her phone—and walked in on him with someone else.

A volunteer.

A girl barely twenty.

Eva didn't scream. She didn't cry.

She just walked out.

And the silence afterward hurt worse than the betrayal.

No one reached out—not the senior pastor, not the leadership team, not even the women who used to call her "sister."

Rumors spread faster than fire.

Some said she had been the jealous one. Others claimed she was "too emotional" to be a leader anyway.

But the final blow?

Noah stayed.

She did not.

He preached the next Sunday with a carefully worded prayer about "seasons of change." He apologized generally. Not publicly. Not personally.

She resigned that week.

Her inbox flooded with condolences and half-hearted blessings, but not one person asked her what really happened.

She left the church. Left the ministry. Left everything that once made her feel like she belonged.

The shame was suffocating.

It wasn't just the betrayal.

It was the implication that she was no longer usable. No longer whole. No longer enough.

Back in the present, Eva pressed her palms into her eyes. Tears threatened to break free, but she forced them back.

She wasn't going to relive that as a victim anymore.

She was here now.

Still standing.

Still His.

She flipped to a blank page in her journal and scrawled across the top:

"What if the shame isn't mine to carry?"

She stared at it, her heart beating faster.

Then the second question came:

"What if Jesus already took it?"

That's what the cross was, wasn't it?

Not just for sin.

But for shame.

The lies. The humiliation. The whispered accusations that had carved scars into her heart.

He took it all.

She reached for her Bible, its edges marked with wear, and turned to Hebrews 12:2:

"…For the joy set before Him, He endured the cross, scorning its shame, and sat down at the right hand of the throne of God."

Scorning its shame.

Eva read the verse again. Then a third time. And something inside her cracked open.

Jesus hadn't just endured the nails.

He endured the shame.

He let people mock Him. Spit on Him. Strip Him bare and hang Him up for all to see. He took on humiliation so she wouldn't have to live under it.

He bore her shame.

So why was she still wearing it like armor?

Eva dropped the pen, closed her eyes, and exhaled a long, shaking breath.

In that moment, she heard Him.

Not audibly. But deep inside.

"You don't have to carry what I already paid for."

Her tears fell freely now—no longer out of pain, but out of the ache that comes from knowing you've believed a lie too long.

She knelt on the rug.

No altar this time. No sanctuary.

Just her floor.

And Jesus.

"God, I'm tired," she whispered. "I'm so tired of dragging this shame behind me. Of measuring myself by the mistake. Of letting what he did define me."

She paused, hands trembling.

"I give it to You. All of it. The humiliation. The silence. The betrayal. The ache of not being defended. I don't want it anymore. If You really bore my shame, then take it. Please. I can't carry it one more day."

The room was still.

But the silence wasn't empty.

It was holy.

She stayed there a long time. Long enough for the tea to cool to nothing. Long enough for the sun to move across the floor.

When she finally rose, her chest felt lighter.

Her heart? Still tender. Still bruised.

But lighter.

Eva reached into the box and placed the ring gently back inside. Then she closed the lid—and stood up.

She didn't need to prove anything to anyone.

She didn't need to vindicate herself.

God knew the truth.

And for the first time in a long while... that was enough.

Chapter 4 – So Much to Give

The sky was still that muted shade between dawn and morning, the kind of light that made the world feel softer, like it hadn't decided whether to wake fully or keep sleeping. Eva stood outside the squat brick building on Ashford Street, clutching a paper cup of coffee like a lifeline.

The sign over the door read:

"Grace Haven – A Shelter for Women and Children"

It wasn't the kind of place you stumbled into by accident. You had to be looking for it, or you had to have nowhere else to go.

Eva had neither excuse.

She wasn't a client here. She wasn't an employee. She was just a woman with too much time and too much ache in her chest—and, if she was honest, a gnawing restlessness she couldn't shake.

The night before, she'd lain awake, staring at the ceiling of her apartment, feeling that same whisper she'd been hearing for weeks:

You still have something to give.

It didn't make sense. She was no one's worship leader anymore. No one's fiancée. No one's "bright young voice for the next generation."

But maybe—just maybe—her calling hadn't died when her platform did.

She took a sip of coffee, squared her shoulders, and stepped inside.

The air was warm, filled with the faint smell of oatmeal and brewed tea. A cluster of women sat at round tables, some chatting quietly, others eating in silence. A few children darted between chairs, their laughter quick and unfiltered.

A woman at the front desk looked up and smiled. Her nametag read MARLENE.

"Can I help you?" she asked, voice calm but curious.

"I was wondering if you needed… volunteers?" Eva's voice felt too loud in the quiet. "I have time. And I can cook, clean, run errands. Whatever you need."

Marlene tilted her head, studying her like she was trying to place her face. "Have you volunteered before?"

Eva hesitated. "Not… here. But I've worked with people. Ministry work. Music."

Marlene's smile deepened. "Well, we don't need a choir, but we do need help with breakfast cleanup. You up for it?"

"Yes," Eva said too quickly, relief settling in her chest.

By mid-morning, she was elbow-deep in sudsy water, scrubbing oatmeal crust from bowls and stacking them to dry. It wasn't glamorous. It wasn't leading worship or standing on a stage. But it was… good.

She could do this without being recognized. Without her past trailing her like a shadow. Without the weight of proving she was "back."

Here, she was just another set of hands.

Halfway through rinsing a tray of spoons, a voice came from behind her.

"You're new."

Eva turned to see a woman about her age, hair pulled into a messy bun, wearing a sweatshirt that read Boston Marathon 2015. She carried a stack of plates toward the drying rack.

"Yeah," Eva said with a small smile. "First day."

"I'm Talia," the woman said, setting the plates down. "I live here. For now."

Eva nodded, unsure how much to ask. "I'm Eva."

Talia's eyes narrowed like she was measuring her. "What made you come here? You one of those church ladies?"

Eva almost laughed. "I guess I used to be."

Talia shrugged. "Well, if you're here to judge, you'll get bored quick. We've all done stuff we're not proud of. You included, I'm guessing."

Eva blinked, caught off guard by the bluntness. But instead of shrinking, she found herself answering honestly.

"Yeah," she said quietly. "I've made mistakes. Big ones."

Talia studied her a moment longer, then smirked. "Good. Means you're real. Real's what we need here."

For the next few hours, Eva moved between the kitchen, the common room, and the storage closet, folding laundry and sorting boxes of donated clothes. It was mindless work, but not meaningless.

She noticed how the women looked at her—not suspiciously, but with a kind of cautious acceptance. Like they were used to people coming in and leaving just as quickly.

By the end of her shift, she was sweaty, her hair had escaped its ponytail, and she smelled faintly of bleach. And yet… she felt lighter.

Marlene thanked her at the door. "Come back tomorrow if you can. We always need hands."

Eva found herself nodding before she'd even thought about it.

That night, she sat at her kitchen table, journal open, pen poised.

I thought serving God had to look a certain way. Microphone in hand. Music swelling. Words polished. But maybe this is it too—scrubbing dishes, folding clothes, making oatmeal for people who need to know they matter. Maybe this is worship.

Her hand stilled over the page as she realized something:

She hadn't thought about Noah all day.

Not once.

Instead, she thought about the woman who had been too shy to ask for seconds at breakfast until Eva offered. She thought about the little girl who handed her a crayon drawing with the word "Thank you" scrawled across the top.

She thought about Talia's blunt honesty, the kind that stripped away pretense in a way church small talk never had.

There was still pain in her story. Still wounds that needed tending. But there was also this—this strange, quiet pull toward something beyond herself.

She still had so much to give.

And maybe… just maybe… God was showing her how.

Chapter 5 – Praying You'll Stay

The smell of cinnamon oatmeal drifted through the kitchen at Grace Haven. Eva stood at the counter, stirring a large pot with a wooden spoon, steam curling into the early morning air. The hum of soft voices floated in from the common room, punctuated by the occasional laugh or the sound of a chair scraping against the floor.

She'd been coming here for almost two weeks now. Same shift. Same small paycheck of gratitude instead of money. And every day, she found herself looking forward to it.

Not because the work was easy—it wasn't. Not because she had something to prove—she'd stopped chasing that.

It was because of her.

Talia.

The first time Eva met her, she'd been all sharp edges and guarded smirks, speaking in clipped sentences as if kindness were a foreign language. But over the past days, something had begun to soften. It happened in small ways—Talia waiting for Eva at the start of her shift, saving her a seat during lunch breaks, swapping sarcastic jokes while folding laundry.

Eva liked her. More than liked her—she felt drawn to her in that quiet, unexplainable way you sometimes feel when you meet someone who's meant to cross your path.

That morning, as Eva ladled oatmeal into bowls, Talia leaned against the counter, her sweatshirt hood up, hair messy from sleep.

"You cook better than half the staff," Talia said with a lazy grin.

Eva smiled. "High praise, coming from someone who lives here."

"Yeah, well, don't let it go to your head." Talia's tone was light, but her eyes lingered on Eva longer than usual, as if she were weighing whether to say more.

"Rough night?" Eva asked gently.

Talia shrugged. "The usual. Bad dreams."

Eva set the spoon down. "Want to talk about them?"

Another shrug. "Not really. But thanks for asking."

They fell into a comfortable silence, the clink of spoons and the sound of chairs scraping the only noise.

When breakfast was ready, the residents filed in. Eva stayed by the counter, watching as Talia sat at a corner table alone.

After a few minutes, she walked over and sat across from her.

Talia raised an eyebrow. "You're not going to sit with the staff?"

"I'm not staff," Eva reminded her. "I'm just… here."

Talia smirked but didn't push her away.

They ate in companionable quiet for a while, until Talia finally spoke.

"You know why I'm here?"

Eva shook her head. "Only if you want to tell me."

"My boyfriend—ex—was bad news. Started out fine. Then came the drinking, the yelling, the hitting. I stayed longer than I should've. By the time I left, I had nothing. No place to go. No one who cared. Grace Haven took me in."

Eva's chest tightened. "I'm sorry."

Talia shrugged. "Don't be. I'm still here, aren't I? I guess that means something."

"It means everything," Eva said quietly.

Talia studied her for a moment. "What about you? Why are you here? And don't say 'to volunteer.'"

Eva hesitated. "I messed up my life. Or… someone messed it up for me. I'm not sure which anymore. I lost the work I loved. Lost a lot of friends. Spent a long time hiding."

Talia tilted her head. "And now?"

"Now…" Eva looked down at her oatmeal. "I'm trying to remember who I am when no one's looking."

Talia didn't answer right away, but her gaze softened.

Later that afternoon, Eva was in the storage room restocking the shelves when she heard a soft sniffle. She turned to see Talia standing in the doorway, arms wrapped around herself.

"You okay?" Eva asked, stepping closer.

Talia shook her head. "I just got a call. My ex is out. He wants to 'talk.'"

Fear rippled through Eva's chest on her friend's behalf.

"Do you have to?" she asked.

Talia laughed bitterly. "I don't want to. But he knows where my mom lives. I can't just ignore it."

Eva didn't think. She just reached out, placing a hand on Talia's arm. "Then we'll pray."

Talia blinked. "Pray? Like… to God?"

"Yes. To God."

Talia hesitated, her jaw tight. "I haven't done that in years. Not since…" She trailed off, shaking her head.

"That's okay," Eva said gently. "You don't have to know what to say. I can say it for both of us."

They sat on two folding chairs in the corner of the storage room, heads bowed, the smell of laundry detergent thick in the air.

Eva's voice was soft but steady:

"God… You see Talia. You see her fear. You see the threats hanging over her. You know her story, her hurt, the battles she's fought just to be here today. I'm asking You—be her refuge. Surround her with Your protection. Let her know she's not alone. And God… please, let her feel safe tonight."

When Eva opened her eyes, Talia's were glistening.

"I didn't think He'd listen to me," Talia whispered.

Eva smiled. "He listens to you more than you think."

That night, lying in bed, Eva replayed the moment over and over. She'd been avoiding prayer for so long—afraid God was tired of hearing from her, ashamed of how long she'd stayed silent. But in that small, detergent-scented storage room, the words had come naturally. Not polished. Not perfect. Just real.

And she realized… she missed it.

Missed talking to Him.

Missed believing He was listening.

So, she prayed again. For Talia. For the women at Grace Haven. For herself.

And when she whispered amen, she felt the faintest stir of something she hadn't felt in years.

Hope.

Chapter 6 – Lord, Please Hear Me

Rain tapped against the window in uneven rhythms, the kind of steady drizzle that blurred the edges of the world outside. Eva sat curled on her couch, a blanket wrapped around her shoulders and her journal balanced on her knees.

It had been weeks since she'd started volunteering at Grace Haven, and for the first time in a long time, she'd been able to push the heaviness of her past into the background. But the quiet of this rainy afternoon pulled it all forward again.

She opened her journal to a blank page.

The pen hovered for a long moment before her hand began to move.

Dear God,

I don't even know where to start. You've heard it all before—my tears, my anger, my endless apologies.

But there's one question I've never really dared to ask out loud.

Can I still be used?

I know what the church said. I know what the people said. I know what my own heart has been saying for years—"No, you've blown it. No, you're too messy. No, you don't get a second chance."

But is that You speaking? Or is that shame pretending to be Your voice?

Because I still feel it, Lord. That stirring. That call. Not to a stage or a microphone—though I loved those things—but to people. To tell them they're seen. That they're loved. That they still matter.

I'm afraid to hope. Afraid to believe You'd still choose me. Afraid that if I try to step into anything again, the whispers will come back louder than before.

But I'm also afraid of staying silent.

So I'm asking… if there's still a place for me in Your plan, will You show me? Will You open a door, even a tiny one, and give me the courage to walk through it?

I don't want to be the girl who hides anymore.

Please hear me.

Amen.

She set the pen down, staring at the page. It wasn't polished. It wasn't poetic. But it was honest.

Eva closed the journal and left it on the coffee table as she got up to make tea. The rain had eased into a soft mist by the time she glanced at the clock. She'd promised to drop off donated coats at the youth center across from Grace Haven before dinner.

The Bridge Youth Center was buzzing when she walked in—teenagers playing ping-pong in the corner, music playing softly over the speakers, and the smell of pizza hanging in the air.

"Drop-off?" a voice called from behind a desk piled with flyers and sports equipment.

Eva smiled. "Yeah. Winter coats. Thought some of your kids might need them."

The man behind the desk came around to help. He was tall, maybe mid-thirties, with warm brown eyes and a hoodie that read "Bridge – Love God. Love People."

"I'm Nate," he said, taking the coats from her arms. "You volunteer at Grace Haven, right?"

Eva blinked. "Yeah, how'd you know?"

"My sister works there. Said there was a new volunteer who was 'different.' Her words, not mine."

Eva laughed softly. "Different good or different bad?"

"Good," Nate said with an easy grin. "She said you actually listen."

Eva felt heat rise to her cheeks. "I try."

As Nate turned to put the coats on a rack, something slipped from between them and fell to the floor.

Eva bent to pick it up—and froze.

Her journal.

She must have tossed it into the bag by accident when she was gathering coats.

Before she could reach for it, Nate leaned down and picked it up. The cover flipped open just enough for him to read the words at the top of the page:

"Can I still be used?"

His expression shifted—softened. "Is this yours?"

"Yes," Eva said quickly, reaching for it.

Nate didn't hand it over right away. "I'm sorry, I didn't mean to see anything. But… that's a question I've heard before. A lot."

Eva hesitated, her journal still halfway between them. "And?"

"And the answer's yes," he said simply. "Every time. No exceptions."

She looked at him, unsure what to say.

Nate glanced at the page again, then closed the journal and handed it back. "If you ever want to talk, I'm around. I work with kids who've been told they're too far gone. I've been there myself. Trust me, God doesn't give up."

Back in her car, Eva sat for a long time with the journal in her lap.

His words echoed in her head: "No exceptions."

It wasn't a divine voice from heaven. It wasn't a booming revelation.

But maybe—just maybe—it was an answer.

A tiny open door.

The kind she'd prayed for.

Chapter 7 – Who I Am

The city was quieter than usual that morning, the streets still wet from last night's rain. Eva sat at a small corner table in Sparrow's Nest Café, hands wrapped around a mug of black coffee that had long since cooled.

She'd been coming here for years, even during her years in hiding. Back then, she would sit with her headphones in, scribbling in her journal, avoiding eye contact with anyone who might know her face.

But today felt different.

Today, the journal lay open on the table, the words from her last prayer staring back at her:

"Can I still be used?"

She tapped the pen against the page, feeling that same quiet stirring she'd felt at Grace Haven, in the youth center with Nate, in the storage room when she prayed for Talia.

It was a feeling she'd been trying to outrun for years.

And she realized why.

Because as long as she stayed hidden—behind her volunteer work, behind her silence—she didn't have to face the fear that maybe she wasn't enough anymore.

But the truth was, shame had been her disguise.

Not healing. Not humility.

Shame.

She started writing again, her pen moving slowly at first, then faster:

I've been hiding behind my shame. Pretending I'm doing it to be humble, but really I'm just afraid. Afraid people will still remember. Afraid they'll judge me all over again. Afraid they'll be right. But God... I think this is who I am. A servant. A singer. Someone who speaks life, even if my voice shakes.

She paused, her eyes blurring.

And if that's still who I am, then I can't keep living like I'm dead.

A chair scraped the floor beside her, and she looked up to see Nate setting his coffee down.

"Hey," he said with an easy smile. "Didn't mean to intrude. This seat taken?"

Eva shook her head. "No, go ahead."

He glanced at her open journal. "You writing?"

She hesitated, then nodded. "Trying to."

"About?"

Eva exhaled, looking out the window at the drizzle. "About who I am. Or who I used to be. Or maybe both."

Nate leaned back in his chair, studying her for a moment. "You ever think those might be the same person? Just… wiser now?"

Eva's lips curved faintly. "I don't know. I feel like I've been split in two—before everything happened, and after."

"Maybe that's not a bad thing," Nate said. "Sometimes God breaks us open so the real us can get out."

His words hit her like a gentle nudge in the ribs—unexpected, but exactly where she needed it.

They talked for nearly an hour, about the youth center, about the women at Grace Haven, about their own stories of loss and recovery.

When Nate got up to leave, he rested a hand briefly on the back of her chair. "You know, if you ever want to share your story with some of our kids, they'd listen. You've got something they need to hear."

Eva's chest tightened. "I'm not ready for that."

He smiled. "Maybe not. But you will be."

That evening, she found herself back at Grace Haven, helping with dinner. The smell of garlic bread filled the kitchen, and laughter spilled in from the dining area.

Talia was setting out plates when Eva joined her. "Busy night?"

"Always," Talia said, rolling her eyes playfully. Then, more softly: "You okay? You look… different."

Eva leaned against the counter, wiping her hands on a towel. "I've been thinking. About who I am. And I realized—I've been hiding behind my shame for a long time."

Talia frowned slightly. "Why?"

"Because it's easier than risking being seen and rejected again," Eva said honestly. "But… I don't want to hide anymore. I'm not just the mistake I made. I'm not just the gossip they spread. I'm still me. I'm still the girl God called years ago. And maybe she's braver than I thought."

Talia's lips curved into a slow smile. "Sounds like you're figuring stuff out."

"Trying to," Eva said, and for the first time in years, the words didn't feel like a cover-up—they felt like truth.

Later that night, in the quiet of her apartment, Eva stood in front of her bathroom mirror. She studied her own reflection, the fine lines around her eyes, the wear in her expression that wasn't there a few years ago.

And then she said it aloud:

"I've been hiding behind my shame. But this is who I am."

Not in defiance. Not in arrogance. But in acceptance.

A servant.
A singer.
A daughter of God.

She let the words settle like roots in soil.

And for the first time in a long time, she didn't just believe she could still be used.

She believed she already was.

Chapter 8 – Save Me, Don't Let Me Stray

Eva was stacking clean dishes in Grace Haven's kitchen when her phone buzzed in her back pocket. She almost ignored it—she'd gotten good at silencing the world outside this building—but something in her spirit nudged her to look.

It was a number she didn't recognize, but the message was short:

Hey Eva, this is Pastor Miriam. Can you call me when you get a minute?

Her pulse quickened. Pastor Miriam never reached out without a reason.

She dried her hands, stepped into the hallway, and called.

"Eva!" Miriam's warm, unhurried voice came through the line. "I hope I'm not catching you at a bad time."

"Not at all," Eva said, though her stomach knotted.

"I'll get right to it," Miriam continued. "We're hosting a special worship night next month. Our music director is on family leave, and I'd like you to co-lead with one of our younger leaders. Just for the night."

The words hit like a wave—both exhilarating and terrifying.

"Miriam… I don't know," Eva said quickly. "It's been years. People still remember what happened. I don't want to cause problems for the church."

"Eva," Miriam's tone was gentle but firm, "I know the past. I also know your heart. And so does God. If He's opening a door, why are you trying to close it?"

Eva pressed her forehead to the wall, eyes squeezed shut. "Because I don't want to walk into a room and see judgment in people's eyes. I don't want to give them another reason to talk."

"Sweetheart," Miriam said softly, "people talked about Jesus, too. And He never let that stop Him from doing the Father's work."

Eva swallowed hard.

"I'm not asking you to prove anything," Miriam continued. "I'm asking you to obey. God's plan doesn't expire because of a rough chapter in our story. If anything, it gets deeper."

After they hung up, Eva stayed in the hallway, staring at the pale green walls. She could already feel the old anxiety creeping in—the what-ifs, the imagined whispers, the fear of standing under those bright lights again.

But beneath the fear… something else stirred.

A longing.

It wasn't about a stage or an audience. It was about worship. About lifting her voice again—not for recognition, but for Him.

And maybe… to finally stand in the place she'd run from for so long.

That night, she sat at her kitchen table with her journal open.

God, You know my fear. You know how small I feel right now. But You also know how much I miss this. If this is from You, save me from my own hesitation. Don't let me stray from Your perfect plan—even if it means walking back into a place I once left in shame.

She stared at the page for a long time, the ink still drying, before closing the journal.

The next day at Grace Haven, she found herself telling Talia about the invitation.

"You're scared," Talia said, leaning against the counter.

"Terrified," Eva admitted. "What if I mess up? What if I freeze? What if people don't think I belong up there?"

Talia smirked. "You think I cared what anyone thought when I walked into this place? I had two black eyes and no plan. People stared. But I showed up anyway. And you—you're telling me you might not show up to do the thing you were born to do?"

Eva blinked. "Born to do?"

"Yeah. I've seen you singing when you think nobody's listening. That's not just a hobby. That's part of you. And if you bury it, you're not just hiding from them—you're hiding from yourself."

Eva didn't know what to say. But she knew Talia was right.

That evening, she sent a message to Pastor Miriam:

I'll do it.

Her finger hovered over "send" for a long moment before she tapped it.

Almost immediately, Miriam replied:

Good. I'll be praying for you every step of the way.

Eva set her phone down and exhaled deeply.

This was happening.

And for the first time in years, the thought of standing on that stage didn't feel like a sentence—it felt like a calling.

Chapter 9 – You Said I Had to Change

The counseling office didn't look the way Eva expected.

She'd pictured something cold and clinical—gray chairs, sterile walls, the faint hum of a clock marking every passing second. Instead, sunlight poured through gauzy curtains onto shelves lined with books and potted plants. A diffuser filled the air with the faint scent of lavender.

The counselor, Dr. Lillian Crane, sat in a wingback chair opposite the couch where Eva hesitated to sit. She was in her late fifties, with kind eyes that didn't try to dissect her before she'd even spoken.

"You must be Eva," Dr. Crane said, gesturing to the seat. "Take your time. We're not in a rush."

Eva sat, fingers twisting in her lap. "Pastor Miriam suggested I come. She said if I'm going to step back into ministry—even just for one night—I should deal with… some things."

Dr. Crane smiled gently. "Do you agree with her?"

Eva hesitated. "I think so. I mean, I've done a lot of praying. But I still feel… stuck. Like there's something under the surface I can't quite get to."

"That's often how it works," Dr. Crane said. "Prayer is powerful. But sometimes God invites us to dig with Him—to get to the root, not just the fruit."

Over the next several weeks, the sessions became a rhythm.

At first, Eva stuck to the safe topics—her work at Grace Haven, her friendship with Talia, her hesitance about the worship night. But Dr. Crane had a way of circling back, gently, until Eva found herself opening doors she hadn't touched in years.

One afternoon, they sat in comfortable silence before Dr. Crane asked, "When was the first time you remember feeling like you had to be perfect?"

The answer rose instantly, unbidden.

"When I was eight."

She told the story in a rush, words spilling out before she could stop them: how she had sung her first solo at church that year, and how afterward her father had smiled, hugged her, and said, "Perfect pitch, baby girl. Don't lose that."

He meant it as praise, but something in her young heart had heard it as a warning: If you mess up, you lose the approval.

From then on, perfection wasn't just a goal—it was the price of love.

Dr. Crane listened without interrupting. "And how did that belief affect the way you saw yourself later?"

Eva stared at the floor. "It made me work harder. But it also made me afraid. Every note, every lyric, every word I spoke from a stage—if it wasn't flawless, I felt like a failure."

As the sessions went on, they moved into deeper waters—how perfectionism had kept her striving in ministry, how it had made Noah's betrayal feel like a public declaration that she wasn't good enough, how shame had fed on that fear until it silenced her.

And beneath all of it, they found something else:

An identity crisis.

Somewhere along the way, Eva had begun to confuse what she did with who she was.

Singing, leading worship, writing songs—those had been gifts God gave her. But she had turned them into the definition of her worth. When those things were taken away, she hadn't just lost her role —she'd lost herself.

One rainy afternoon, Dr. Crane leaned forward. "Eva, if you never sang again—if you never stood on another stage—would you still believe God loved you the same?"

Eva's throat tightened. "I want to say yes. But I don't know if I believe it yet."

"That's okay," Dr. Crane said. "That's why you're here. Change doesn't happen in a moment—it happens in the choosing. Over and over."

Eva thought about that long after the session ended.

That night, back in her apartment, she wrote in her journal:

God, You said I had to change, and I've been trying. But I think I misunderstood. I thought I had to fix myself—make myself flawless before You could use me again. Now I see You're asking for something harder: to believe I'm Yours even when I'm not perfect. Even when I fail. Even when the world remembers my worst day.

She set the pen down, pressing her palm against the page like she could seal the words there.

She wasn't "fixed" yet. She wasn't sure she ever would be. But she was learning that maybe God wasn't waiting for perfection.

Maybe He was just waiting for surrender.

Chapter 10 – My Soul's Not Dying

The Bible on Eva's coffee table was heavier than it looked.

Not in weight—it was a slim, well-worn study Bible with curled page edges and underlined verses—but in memory. It had been years since she'd opened it without feeling that knot of guilt in her stomach, years since she'd read the words for herself and not for a worship set, a sermon, or a song lyric.

She sat cross-legged on the couch, journal and pen beside her, coffee cooling in the mug she hadn't touched.

The apartment was silent except for the soft hum of the fridge.

Eva ran her hand over the leather cover and whispered, "Okay. No more avoiding You."

She started in the Psalms.

Not with an agenda. Not to prepare a song. Just to listen.

Her eyes fell on Psalm 73:26:

"My flesh and my heart may fail, but God is the strength of my heart and my portion forever."

The words hit something deep.

Her flesh had failed. Her heart had failed. She'd walked away from her calling, let bitterness take root, let shame define her. But God is the strength of my heart—not my talent, not my performance, not the opinions of the crowd.

Her chest loosened as she read it again.

For the next hour, she moved slowly through the pages. The Scriptures felt alive again—sharp and warm at the same time, like sunlight through stained glass.

She read Isaiah 43:19:

"See, I am doing a new thing! Now it springs up; do you not perceive it?"

A new thing.

Not a recycled thing. Not a patched-up thing.

New.

Her eyes blurred with tears, and she found herself whispering, "Do it in me, God. Please. Do something new in me."

That night, she didn't turn on the TV.

Instead, she pulled out her guitar from the closet, the one that had been gathering dust since she'd stopped leading worship. The strings were a little out of tune, but her fingers still remembered the chords.

She started softly, almost afraid of her own voice.

First, it was fragments of old worship songs—melodies she hadn't touched in years. Then, slowly, she began to sing new words. Words she hadn't planned, words that rose up out of the Scriptures she'd read earlier.

You are my portion / You are my strength
Even in shadows / You give me breath
You are the new thing / Breaking the ground
My soul's not dying / I'm rising now

Her voice cracked on the last line, but she didn't stop.

She played until her fingers ached, until her living room felt less like a lonely apartment and more like a sanctuary.

She didn't realize how much she'd missed this—worship that wasn't about the arrangement or the audience or the perfect high note. Worship that was just for Him.

When she finally set the guitar down, she sat on the floor, leaning against the couch, and prayed:

"God… thank You for not letting me stay dead inside. I thought I lost everything when I walked away, but maybe I was just buried. And You… You're the one pulling me back into the light."

It wasn't a dramatic moment. No thunder. No flash of divine light.

Just peace.

And the quiet, certain sense that she was coming alive again.

By the end of the week, this had become her routine:

Morning coffee. Psalms or Isaiah. A few pages in her journal. Evening guitar sessions where the songs spilled out unpolished but honest.

Some nights she laughed at herself when she forgot lyrics or hit the wrong chord. Other nights she sang until her voice went hoarse.

And every time, she felt it.

The stirring.

The warmth in her chest that reminded her she wasn't just surviving anymore.

Her soul wasn't dying.

It was waking up.

Chapter 11 – In You I'm Stronger

The lights in the small fellowship hall were warm, casting a soft glow over the crowd gathered for Grace Haven's annual benefit dinner. The tables were dressed in white linens, each centerpiece a simple mason jar of wildflowers. Laughter mingled with the quiet clink of silverware.

Eva stood in the corner near the stage, palms damp, guitar strap slung over her shoulder. Her heart thudded in her chest—not with excitement, but with the raw, electric charge of stepping into something she hadn't done in years.

It wasn't a concert. It wasn't even a church service. Just a room full of people—staff, residents, volunteers—celebrating another year of second chances.

And yet, for Eva, it felt like the biggest stage of her life.

She could hear the emcee wrapping up the introduction:

"…and tonight, we have a special treat. One of our volunteers, someone whose kindness and quiet spirit have blessed us deeply, is going to share a song. Please welcome… Eva Hart."

The applause was polite but warm.

Her feet felt like they were made of lead as she crossed to the mic stand. She adjusted it slowly, stalling for time.

"Hi," she began, her voice catching slightly. "I haven't done this in… well, a long time. But this place—Grace Haven—has reminded me what it means to have hope. And I wanted to share a song that came out of that."

She glanced at the guitar in her hands, fingers finding the first chord.

The opening notes were soft, almost tentative, but the sound filled the room.

She began to sing:

You are my portion / You are my strength
Even in shadows / You give me breath

Her voice was low at first, like she was singing only to herself. But then something shifted.

She thought of the Psalms she'd been reading. The prayers she'd whispered over Talia. The journal pages filled with questions and quiet surrender.

Her voice lifted.

You are the new thing / Breaking the ground
My soul's not dying / I'm rising now

The air in the room changed. Conversations stilled. Forks clinked against plates and then went silent. Even the restless shifting of chairs stopped.

Eva felt her chest open as the words poured out—not from muscle memory, but from a place so deep it felt like God Himself was breathing them through her.

In You I'm stronger / I'm not who I was
In You I'm standing / I'm held by Your love

Her fingers moved fluidly over the strings, the notes ringing pure and warm.

By the second verse, she wasn't thinking about her voice anymore. She wasn't wondering who might be judging her. She was lost in the worship—just her, her guitar, and the One she was singing to.

And then she looked up.

She saw Marlene from the front desk, tears streaming silently down her cheeks. A teenage boy she recognized from the youth center had his head bowed, lips moving in quiet prayer. Two women from the shelter were holding hands, swaying gently.

This wasn't a performance.

This was ministry.

And it had nothing to do with her polish or her pitch.

It was the cracks in her—her story, her pain—that were letting the light through.

By the final chorus, her voice swelled:

In You I'm stronger / I'm not who I was
In You I'm standing / I'm held by Your love
You lift my head / You make me new
I'm stronger, Lord… in You

The last chord lingered in the air like a breath held between heartbeats. She let it fade naturally, the sound dissolving into a deep, sacred silence.

Then, as if on cue, the room erupted into applause—not the quick, polite kind, but something raw. Genuine. Some people stood. Others wiped their eyes.

Eva smiled, but it wasn't the stage-smile she used to wear. It was small, real, and tinged with awe.

After she stepped down, Talia was the first to find her. She didn't say anything, just wrapped her in a hug that nearly lifted her off her feet.

"That," Talia whispered, "was the real you."

Eva pulled back, blinking. "What do you mean?"

"I mean," Talia said, "that's the version of you that doesn't care who's watching. The version that remembers why she started in the first place."

On her way out that night, Eva found herself whispering another prayer, one she hadn't prayed in years—not to be used again, not to be put back on a stage, but simply:

"God… thank You. For letting me remember."

She didn't need the spotlight.

But she knew, deep in her bones, that her voice—her life—still had purpose.

And maybe… this was only the beginning.

Chapter 12 – Through the Fire

The invitation came in the form of a text from Nate.

Big youth revival at the Bridge next month. Want you to share your story and maybe sing?

Eva stared at the message, her stomach flipping.

A song, maybe.
Her story?
That was different.

Singing felt safe now—it let her pour out her heart without giving away too much. But standing in front of a room full of teenagers and telling them the parts of her life she still winced to remember? That felt like walking into a burning building with no way out.

She typed a quick reply:

I don't think I'm ready for that.

Her finger hovered over "send."

But she didn't press it.

Instead, she set the phone down and went to make tea.

All day, the thought followed her.

She imagined the questions—the raised eyebrows, the whispered Isn't she the one who…?

She imagined tripping over her words, leaving out too much, saying too much.

But she also imagined something else.

She imagined one girl, sitting in the back row, carrying the same shame Eva had carried for years. She imagined that girl hearing: Your mistakes don't disqualify you. You can start over.

By the time the sun dipped behind the buildings, Eva was pacing her living room.

"God," she muttered, "are You really asking me to do this? You know I'm still healing. You know this could hurt. What if I mess it up?"

The silence was deep, but it wasn't empty.

A verse from Isaiah rose in her mind like a flame:

"When you walk through the fire, you will not be burned; the flames will not set you ablaze."

Eva closed her eyes. "Through the fire," she whispered.

The next morning, she texted Nate back:

Okay. I'll do it. But I'm trusting God to get me through.

The night of the revival, the air outside the Bridge Youth Center buzzed with energy. Inside, the room pulsed with music—drums, bass, voices singing so loud they shook the floor.

Eva stood in the wings, hands clasped so tightly her knuckles were white. Nate's voice came through the mic:

"Next, we've got someone who knows what it's like to walk through tough seasons and come out stronger. She's a friend of ours, and I think you're going to see why she's here tonight. Please welcome, Eva Hart."

The applause was loud, but Eva heard her own heartbeat above it.

She stepped out into the light.

It was brighter than she expected, the stage lights turning the crowd into a blur of faces. She gripped the mic, forcing herself to breathe.

"I… um… I used to think I had to be perfect for God to love me," she began. "And for a while, I thought I was. Until I wasn't."

She told them about the betrayal. The whispers. The shame. Not in graphic detail, but enough to paint the picture. Enough to let them see her humanity.

And then she told them about Grace Haven. About Talia. About the way God had quietly, persistently drawn her back through Scripture, worship, and unexpected friendships.

"I thought my story was over," she said, voice steady now. "But God was just rewriting it."

The room was silent, the kind of silence that wasn't disinterest—it was listening.

Eva set the mic in the stand and reached for her guitar.

"I wrote this song in my living room, when I realized I wasn't dead inside anymore," she said. "It's called In You I'm Stronger."

The first chord rang out clear and warm.

Her voice carried over the crowd, filling every corner of the room.

In You I'm stronger / I'm not who I was
In You I'm standing / I'm held by Your love

It wasn't just music—it was testimony. The kind you could feel in your bones.

When she finished, the applause came like a wave, but what mattered wasn't the sound—it was the sight of teenagers at the altar, some with heads bowed, others with hands lifted, tears cutting tracks down their cheeks.

Afterward, one girl—maybe sixteen—found her in the hallway.

"You don't know me," the girl said, "but… I've been thinking about ending it. Because I thought I'd messed up too bad for God to want me. But hearing you… I think maybe I can start over."

Eva's throat tightened. She hugged the girl, whispering, "You can. You absolutely can."

As the girl walked away, Eva leaned against the wall, her eyes stinging.

"Through the fire," she murmured. "You got me through."

Chapter 13 – Don't Let Go of My Hand

The sanctuary lights were low, a soft golden hue spilling across the stage. A hush had settled over the crowd—youth, adults, volunteers—faces lifted toward her. Eva stood with the mic in her hand, guitar slung across her shoulder, the edges of her paper-thin notes trembling in her fingers.

This wasn't just another worship set. Tonight, Nate had asked her to share her testimony again—only this time, she was to go deeper.

She had prayed all week for the right words. She'd asked God to make her brave. But now, with every pair of eyes fixed on her, her throat tightened and her rehearsed introduction scattered like ash.

She took a deep breath.

"I thought I was coming here tonight to tell you how God fixed me," she began, voice steady but low. "But that's not really the truth. The truth is… I'm still in process. I'm still learning how to trust Him. I'm still fighting days when the shame tries to crawl back in."

A flicker of unease moved through her—had she just said too much?

The room stayed still, waiting.

"I used to think God's love was fragile," she continued. "Like if I broke too badly, He'd just… let go. But I've learned something in the fire, in the quiet, in the nights when all I could pray was 'Please don't let go of my hand.'"

Her voice wavered, and she looked down, blinking hard. "And He never did."

Her chest heaved once, and the tears came—hot and unstoppable. She tried to keep going, but the lump in her throat swelled. Her fingers faltered on the guitar strings. The words blurred on the page in front of her.

A year ago, she would have panicked. She would have stepped off the stage, humiliated, convinced she'd ruined everything.

But tonight… she didn't run.

She let the silence breathe.

She let them see her exactly as she was—shaking, tear-streaked, voice cracking under the weight of her own story.

Because the truth was, she wasn't standing there in spite of her brokenness. She was standing because of it.

And in that silence, she felt it.

The Spirit.

Not in a thunderclap, not in a rush of sound—but like a steady hand on her back, holding her upright.

It was as if God Himself whispered, "This is the moment. This is why I brought you here. Not to impress them. To remind them—and you—that I'm the one holding you."

Eva looked up, meeting the faces in the crowd. She set the guitar aside and stepped closer to the edge of the stage.

"I'm not going to pretend this is easy," she said, her voice shaking but clear now. "But I want you to know—whatever you've been through, whatever you've done, whatever's been done to you—He hasn't let go. Even if you feel like you're barely hanging on, His grip is stronger."

Heads nodded. Some eyes closed. A few hands lifted.

She picked the guitar back up, strummed the opening chord of In You I'm Stronger, and began to sing—soft at first, like a prayer:

You lift my head / You make me new
I'm stronger, Lord… in You

By the second chorus, the crowd was singing with her. The voices rose together, filling the room until she could barely hear her own.

And in that sea of sound, her fear dissolved.

She wasn't standing alone anymore.

When the final note faded, she didn't feel drained. She felt… free.

Because tonight hadn't been about a flawless delivery. It hadn't been about performing.

It had been about telling the truth—and letting God hold her through it.

And she knew, walking off that stage, that no matter where this journey took her next, she could keep praying the same words without fear of the answer:

Don't let go of my hand.

Chapter 14 – I Walk by Faith

The note was sitting on Eva's pillow when she got home from her shift at Grace Haven.

Her first thought was that she'd left something behind at the shelter and Marlene had dropped it off. But when she unfolded the paper, her breath caught.

It was from Talia.

Eva,

I didn't want to say goodbye in person because I knew you'd try to talk me out of this. I'm going back to rehab. Not because I failed, but because I want to win—for real this time.

You've been one of the first people in years to look me in the eye and see me, not just my mistakes. You've prayed for me when I didn't believe it would do any good. You've shown me that maybe God hasn't given up on me, even when I gave up on myself.

Don't stop doing what you do. Even if it feels small, it's not. You planted something in me.

I'll write when I can.

—Talia

Eva read the letter twice, her eyes stinging by the second read. She sat down on the edge of the bed, running her fingers over the creases in the paper like it could anchor her friend there.

Part of her wanted to cry for the loss—the empty chair at breakfast, the missing banter in the laundry room, the way Talia's presence had filled the space with a kind of gritty honesty Eva had come to depend on.

But a bigger part of her… felt proud.

Talia was choosing the harder road. The one that required surrender.

The one Eva herself had been walking in her own way.

That night, Eva carried the letter into the living room and laid it open beside her Bible. She turned to Hebrews 11, the chapter on faith, and read:

"Now faith is confidence in what we hope for and assurance about what we do not see."

She closed her eyes.

"God… I can't see where she's going. I can't walk it for her. But I trust You. And I trust the seeds You've planted in her."

Over the next week, Eva kept the letter tucked in her journal. On mornings when the doubts came— about her own calling, about her worth—she would read Talia's words again.

Don't stop doing what you do.

It became a kind of quiet mantra, pulling her forward when she felt the weight of uncertainty pressing down.

At the end of the week, Pastor Miriam called to finalize the worship night details.

"We've confirmed the setlist," Miriam said. "You'll co-lead the last two songs with Jeremy. And I'd like you to share something short before we close."

Eva hesitated. "You mean… speak?"

"Yes," Miriam said with a smile in her voice. "Doesn't have to be long. Just something from the heart. You've been through fire, Eva. Don't underestimate what that testimony can do."

Her pulse quickened. She thought of Talia, of the way God had used their friendship to pull her back into prayer, into faith, into hope.

Maybe it was time to take another step forward.

That night, Eva stood at her window, looking out over the city. The streetlights blinked on, one by one, like small promises in the dark.

"I don't see the whole road," she whispered. "But I'll walk it anyway."

And in that moment, she understood—faith wasn't waiting until you had every answer.

It was taking the next step with an open hand.

Chapter 15 – I Understand

The city had gone quiet.

It was one of those nights where the air was so still, you could hear the hum of the streetlights through the closed windows. Eva sat cross-legged on the floor of her apartment, a single candle flickering on the coffee table. Her Bible lay open to the Psalms, her journal beside it.

She hadn't planned on staying up late. But something in her spirit wouldn't let her go to bed. It was as if God had been nudging her all evening: Sit with Me.

So she did.

She closed her eyes and breathed in slow, deep pulls of air. The candlelight painted her walls in warm, trembling gold. Outside, a soft drizzle tapped against the glass—gentle, rhythmic, like a heartbeat.

She began to pray in a whisper, words slow and unhurried.

"God… I don't want to just believe in Your grace. I want to understand it. I want to live in it. But I keep asking myself—why did I have to go through all that? The betrayal, the shame, the silence? Why let me wander so far into the wilderness?"

The rain outside grew steadier, a hushed percussion.

She waited. Not for a booming answer, but for the small, quiet kind—the kind she had learned was His way of speaking to her.

In her mind's eye, she saw it:

She was standing in a wide, barren desert. The sun was fierce, the wind dry. Her hands were empty, her throat parched. In the distance, she could see the life she used to have—green fields, water, people she loved—but it was separated from her by miles of wasteland.

She turned in a slow circle, looking for a way out, but there was nothing.

And then… she noticed something she hadn't before.

A stream. Small, almost hidden, trickling out from a crack in a rock.

She knelt beside it, cupping the water in her hands, and as she drank, she felt something shift—not just in her body, but in her soul.

It was enough to keep her going one more day.

And then another.

Day after day, she came back to that stream. Sometimes it was all she had.

The vision faded, and she was back in her living room. The candle's flame wavered, and she realized she was crying—not the hot, angry tears of the past, but tears that felt… clean.

It hit her like a gentle wave:

You had to go through the wilderness so you could learn where the water comes from.

The words were clear in her spirit, ringing with truth.

If she'd stayed in the green fields, she might have thought the blessing was the grass, the comfort, the people. But in the desert, she learned that the real source—the stream—was Him.

The grace wasn't the good season. The grace was His presence in the barren one.

She whispered into the quiet, "I understand."

Not everything. Not all the why's or how's. But she understood enough.

Enough to see that the wilderness hadn't been punishment—it had been preparation. It had stripped away her illusions and left her with the one thing that could never be taken: the love of a God who never let her go.

She leaned back against the couch, the rain still tapping against the glass, and for the first time in years, she felt not just relief… but gratitude.

Because she'd found the stream.

And she would never forget where to find it again.

Chapter 16 – We Walk So Far

The phone call came on a Tuesday afternoon.

Eva was folding laundry in her apartment, the kind of mindless chore that left plenty of room for her thoughts to drift, when her phone buzzed with a number she hadn't seen in years.

Her father.

For a moment, she just stared at the screen, her hands frozen over a stack of clean towels. She hadn't spoken to him in nearly a decade—not since the argument that fractured what little was left of their relationship.

She almost let it go to voicemail.

Almost.

"Hello?" Her voice was tentative, like she wasn't sure if she wanted to be heard.

"Eva." His voice was deeper than she remembered, slower too, like every word had to push through something heavy. "It's… been a while."

"Yes," she said simply.

There was a long pause. Then: "I heard you've been singing again."

Eva frowned. "From who?"

"An old friend from the church."

Another pause, this one heavier. "I was wondering if we could meet. Just to talk."

Her mind immediately filled with old wounds—the disapproval, the way he'd used words like failure and disappointment when she left home to pursue ministry instead of a "real career," the silence after her scandal, as if she'd embarrassed him by existing.

But somewhere underneath the instinct to say no was a quieter voice, the one that had been growing stronger lately. The one that said healing sometimes starts with a step you don't want to take.

"Okay," she heard herself say. "Where?"

They met at a small park near the river, where the trees leaned over the walking path like they were trying to listen in.

He was already sitting on a bench when she arrived, wearing the same kind of jacket he'd worn when she was a little girl—dark wool, collar turned up against the wind. His hair was grayer, his face lined, but his eyes were the same.

"Hi," she said, stopping a few feet away.

He stood, hesitant, then gestured for her to sit. "You look… well."

"Thanks." She kept her hands folded in her lap, unsure where to put her gaze.

They talked in fits and starts at first—safe topics. Weather. How the city had changed. The fact that he still worked at the same place.

But eventually, he cleared his throat. "Eva, I owe you an apology. I wasn't there when you needed me. I didn't call. I didn't defend you. I… thought I was teaching you to be strong by making you handle it alone. But all I did was abandon you."

The words hung in the cool air between them.

Eva's eyes stung. "Do you know how far I had to walk alone?" she asked, her voice trembling. "How far it felt from the little girl who wanted to make you proud?"

"I do now," he said quietly. "We walk so far from each other sometimes… it feels impossible to get back. But I'm here now. If you'll let me be."

She looked at him for a long moment.

She could hold on to the anger. She could punish him by keeping the distance. It would be easier than opening the door to the possibility of being hurt again.

But she thought of the wilderness vision God had given her. The stream. The grace she'd received when she didn't deserve it.

And she realized—this was her chance to offer the same.

"I forgive you," she said softly. "Not because it didn't hurt, but because I'm tired of carrying it."

Something in his shoulders loosened, and for the first time, his smile reached his eyes.

They walked along the river for another hour, not as strangers, not quite as father and daughter—but as two people trying to close the distance between them.

When they parted, he hugged her for the first time in years.

It wasn't perfect. It didn't erase the past.

But it was a step.

And sometimes, she thought as she watched him walk away, that's all faith really is—taking the next step, even when you can't see how far the road goes.

Chapter 17 – You Show Us Who We Are

The dream came like a sunrise—slow, but unstoppable.

Eva was standing in an open field, the grass tall enough to brush against her fingertips. A warm wind moved through it in waves, and somewhere in the distance, she could hear singing—not words, just a melody that felt both familiar and impossibly ancient.

She looked down and saw she was wearing white—not the blinding, impossible kind, but simple linen, clean and soft. Her feet were bare, and when she moved, the earth under them felt alive.

Ahead, a figure approached. Not rushing, not looming—just walking toward her with steady purpose.

When He was close enough for her to see His eyes, she stopped breathing.

They weren't the kind of eyes that looked at you. They looked into you. And yet, there was no condemnation there—only recognition, like He was seeing something she'd forgotten was hers.

"You are mine," Jesus said. His voice wasn't loud, but it rolled through her like thunder through the ground. "And you've always been mine."

Tears blurred her vision. "But I lost who I was."

He shook His head gently. "You can't lose what I gave you. Your identity isn't earned—it's revealed. And it's revealed in Me."

She woke with her pillow damp from tears, the words still echoing in her chest. For a long moment, she lay there in the dim morning light, letting the dream settle into her like seeds into soil.

Then she reached for her journal.

Identity isn't earned—it's revealed in Jesus. That's why the shame couldn't erase it. That's why the wilderness couldn't destroy it. I didn't have to claw my way back to who I was. He handed it back to me.

That afternoon, Eva called her father.

"Could I stop by?" she asked.

He sounded surprised, but said yes.

When she arrived, he was in the small kitchen of his apartment, making coffee. He looked up, a flicker of hesitation in his expression—like he wasn't sure if her visit was for good news or bad.

"I had a dream last night," she said as she sat at the table. "It reminded me of something I need to tell you."

He poured the coffee, then sat across from her, waiting.

"I've already told you I forgive you," she continued. "But I realized something. Forgiveness isn't just letting go of the hurt. It's also giving back what distance tried to take away—identity. You're still my dad. That hasn't changed. And I don't want either of us to keep living like it has."

His hands trembled slightly as he set down his mug. "Eva…" His voice cracked, and he cleared his throat. "I don't deserve that."

"Neither do I," she said softly. "That's the point."

They talked for over an hour—not about the past, not about what had gone wrong, but about who they were now, and what they wanted to build going forward.

When she left, she hugged him longer than she had in years.

Walking back to her car, the wind picked up, tugging at her hair. It felt like the same wind from the dream—warm, alive, carrying a song she couldn't quite hear but knew by heart.

She smiled through the tears.

Because she understood now.

Jesus had shown her who she was.

And it was enough.

Chapter 18 – Let Your Love Light the Way

It started with a single post.

Eva hadn't planned on creating anything public. Her journal was private, her prayers whispered in the stillness of her apartment or into the rafters of Grace Haven's kitchen. But one evening, after reading through a page of reflections she'd written on forgiveness and identity, she felt the nudge: Share it.

She hesitated. The internet had never been a safe place for her, especially when the scandal first broke. But the nudge didn't fade.

So she opened her laptop, created a free blog under the title "Worship From the Ashes", and typed out her reflection—word for word, just as she had written it. She ended it with a simple line:

If you're reading this and you think you've walked too far to be found, I promise you—He still knows where you are.

She hit "publish," closed the laptop, and didn't think much more about it.

By the next morning, her phone was buzzing with notifications. Comments, shares, private messages.

A woman from Arizona wrote, "I found this at 2 a.m. when I couldn't sleep. I'm in tears. Thank you for reminding me I'm not lost."

A man from South Africa messaged, "Your words felt like they were written for me. I haven't been in a church in 12 years, but now I'm thinking about going back."

Eva stared at the screen, stunned. She'd expected maybe a handful of people to read it—friends, maybe a few Grace Haven volunteers. But these were strangers. People thousands of miles away.

And somehow, God had put her words in their path.

Encouraged, she began to post weekly. Sometimes it was short—just a verse and a few lines of reflection. Other times it was a longer piece about the wilderness, identity, or grace.

She didn't write like a preacher. She wrote like a friend over coffee, telling you the truth she'd learned the hard way.

The responses grew. People began sharing her posts in their own churches, on their own feeds. A youth group leader from another state asked if they could read one aloud during a retreat.

Eva kept thinking of the dream, of Jesus saying, "Your identity isn't earned—it's revealed in Me." She realized this was part of that identity—not just singing about Him, but speaking what He'd shown her.

One evening, after posting a piece about letting go of shame, she got a message that stopped her cold.

From: Talia

Hey. They let me use the computer at the rehab center. I found your blog. I'm not surprised—it sounds like you. It's good. I'm proud of you. Keep writing. People need this.

Eva read it twice, then pressed her hand to her mouth to hold back the sudden wave of tears.

God was not only using her words to reach strangers—He was using them to keep speaking into Talia's life, even from a distance.

One Saturday morning, Pastor Miriam stopped her after church.

"I've been reading your blog," Miriam said, smiling. "Eva, do you realize what's happening? You're ministering to people all over the world without leaving your kitchen table."

Eva laughed softly, shaking her head. "I'm just telling my story."

"That's what ministry is," Miriam replied. "Letting His love light the way—for you and for them."

That night, Eva sat at her desk, a blank post page open on her laptop. She typed a single sentence at the top:

Lord, let Your love light the way through my words.

She didn't know how long she would keep the blog going. She didn't have a five-year plan, or even a one-year plan.

But she knew this: as long as God kept giving her words, she would keep setting them out like lanterns in the dark.

Because sometimes, one small light was enough to show someone the road home.

Chapter 19 – Boldly Say

The email sat in her inbox like a challenge.

Subject line: Recording Opportunity – Worship Single

Eva hovered her mouse over it for nearly a full minute before clicking.

Hi Eva,

We've been following your blog and some of the clips from your recent worship nights. There's something raw and authentic in your voice—and your words—that we believe would resonate deeply.

We're working on a new worship compilation album with a handful of artists from across the country. Would you consider recording one of your originals for it?

If interested, we'd love to schedule a call this week.

Blessings,
Daniel Matthews
A&R Director, RiverLight Music

She read it twice. Then a third time.

Her gut reaction was No.

Not because she didn't want to sing. Not because she didn't believe in the songs God had given her.

But because she remembered the last time she'd been in a recording studio—the pressure, the whispered criticism, the unspoken competition, and the way one mistake felt like proof she didn't belong there.

She closed the email and set her laptop aside. "Not me," she muttered. "Not now."

The next day at Grace Haven, she mentioned it to Pastor Miriam in passing.

"They want me to record a worship single," Eva said, folding a stack of freshly laundered towels. "But I can't. I'm not ready for that kind of spotlight again."

Miriam tilted her head. "Is it the spotlight you're avoiding, or the past you're still holding onto?"

Eva froze mid-fold.

Miriam stepped closer. "Eva, God's redemption isn't partial. When He restores, He doesn't just give you back what you lost—He multiplies it. If He's opening a door, it's because He's prepared you to walk through it."

That night, Eva sat at her desk with her Bible open to Joel 2:25:

"I will restore to you the years that the locust has eaten."

She read it out loud, the words steady in the quiet.

Maybe the studio wasn't the enemy. Maybe it was the place where the years of silence and shame could be replaced with something new.

She thought of the girl in the back row at the revival, the one who said she'd wanted to give up. She thought of the comments on her blog from people who had never met her but felt seen in her words.

If she said no to this, what message was she sending? That God could redeem some things, but not this?

She opened her laptop again and read the email one more time.

This time, she imagined it—not the nerves, but the moment the music swelled in her headphones and her voice rose, not for perfection, not for industry approval, but for Him.

She imagined singing the truth she'd lived: that grace was bigger, love was stronger, and redemption was real.

Her fingers hovered over the keyboard, then began to type.

Hi Daniel,

Thank you for reaching out. I'd love to talk more about the project.

Blessings,
Eva Hart

When she hit "send," she exhaled—slow, deep, steady.

It wasn't confidence in herself that carried her forward. It was confidence in the One who had brought her from ashes to this moment.

She whispered into the stillness, "God, You redeem. Let this be Yours."

And for the first time in years, the thought of stepping into a studio didn't feel like walking into an old battlefield.

It felt like walking into victory.

Chapter 20 – Stand Tall

The air inside the auditorium pulsed with anticipation. Hundreds of people filled the seats, their voices a low hum of conversation and laughter as the worship band tuned instruments and ran final checks.

From her spot backstage, Eva could see the glow of the stage lights reflecting off the rows of faces. It wasn't a stadium, but the room felt alive—like the air itself was expectant.

She gripped the microphone in both hands, trying to quiet the thud of her heartbeat. Tonight wasn't just another worship night. Tonight, she was debuting Here's Where I Stand—a song born out of journal pages soaked in tears, nights of wrestling with God, and the slow miracle of restoration.

Her voice wasn't at its most polished tonight. She knew that. But she also knew—this wasn't about polish.

This was about truth.

The band leader gave her a nod.

The first chord rang out—clean, warm, reverberating in the stillness.

Eva stepped forward, the stage lights bathing her in gold. She closed her eyes and let the first line fall from her lips:

Here in the dark, I come before You
Jesus, I lift up my hands…

The words were soft, almost a whisper at first, but the room leaned in. She could feel it.

Her voice wasn't flawless—there was a huskiness at the edges, a tremor that betrayed the weight of the lyrics—but it carried something richer than perfection: the pulse of lived experience.

The drums entered, a slow heartbeat under the melody, and she opened her eyes.

Faces blurred in the lights, but she could see movement—hands lifting, shoulders swaying, heads bowed.

She moved into the chorus, her voice growing stronger:

Here's where I stand, here's who I am
Save me, but don't let me stray from Your perfect plan…

The harmony vocals rose behind her, weaving through the melody like threads of light.

By the bridge, she could feel it—the shift. That moment in worship when the line between stage and congregation dissolves and you're all standing in the same place before Him.

She stepped back from the mic for a moment and let the crowd's voices take over:

I walk by faith… I understand…

The sound swelled, raw and unpolished, hundreds of voices singing the truth like they meant it. It wrapped around her, lifting her higher.

She stepped back in, her voice breaking slightly but carrying through:

With Your grace, Lord, I'll make it through…

By the final chorus, she was singing with everything in her. Not caring if her voice cracked, not caring about the tears streaming down her face.

It wasn't performance—it was surrender.

Here's where I stand, here's who I am
Love me, use me, lead me too…
And I'll make it through…

The last note lingered in the air, trembling, as if the room itself didn't want to let it go.

And then came the silence—the holy kind.

When the applause finally broke out, Eva stepped back, clutching the mic at her side. She didn't feel triumphant. She felt… emptied. Poured out.

But in that emptiness was something else—fullness. Peace.

Because she had stood here tonight, not in the shadow of her past, but in the light of her redemption.

She had stood tall.

And she knew, deep in her bones, that this was exactly where she was meant to be.

Chapter 21 – I Am Counted

The first letter arrived in a plain white envelope, postmarked from a small town Eva had never heard of. Inside was a single sheet of lined paper, the handwriting neat but a little shaky.

Dear Eva,

I was at the worship night where you sang Here's Where I Stand. I came with my cousin, not really wanting to be there. I've been in church my whole life, but lately I've felt like I'm drowning.

When you shared about your mistakes and how you thought God couldn't use you anymore, I started crying. It's like you were telling my story.

I just wanted you to know—your honesty saved me that night. I decided not to give up. I'm going to keep walking.

Thank you for standing so I could, too.

Love,
Claire

Eva sat at her kitchen table for a long time after reading it, the letter trembling slightly in her hands.

She thought back to all the nights she'd begged God in private: Does this pain even have a purpose? And now—here was an answer, written in ink by a stranger.

The letters kept coming. Some by email, others handwritten.

One was from a college student who had been battling depression. Another from a single mom who had left an abusive relationship and was afraid she would never belong anywhere again.

They all said different things, but the heartbeat was the same: Your honesty showed me I'm not alone.

One afternoon, she spread them out on her coffee table—pages and pages, voices from every corner of the country.

She ran her fingers over the words, her eyes catching on phrases: "I felt seen." … "God isn't done with me." … "You gave me permission to worship broken."

Tears blurred the ink.

She whispered, "I am counted."

Not for numbers, not for charts or sales or applause. Counted in the way heaven counts—by the hearts reached, the souls encouraged, the chains broken in quiet rooms.

Counted by the God who had never lost track of her, even when she'd lost track of herself.

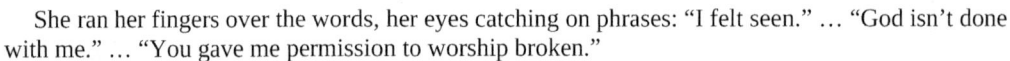

That night, she placed all the letters in a wooden keepsake box. She tucked a small card inside, on which she wrote:

Here's where I stand: I am counted—by God, and by those He sends my way.

And for the first time, she didn't just believe she had been restored. She believed she had been redeemed for a reason.

Chapter 22 – I'm Counting on You

The email came in on a Wednesday morning.

Eva almost didn't open it right away—her mind was already crowded with the week's schedule: a midweek Bible study, volunteer shifts at the shelter, and a songwriting session with the band.

But when she finally clicked it open, the subject line froze her:

Full-Time Worship Director Position – Prayerful Consideration

The message was from Pastor James of New Hope Fellowship, a church she had visited a few times in the past year. They were looking for someone to lead their worship ministry—not just for Sunday services, but to shepherd the creative team, mentor younger musicians, and help cultivate a deeper culture of worship in the congregation.

We've prayed over this role for months, he wrote, and your name kept coming up in conversations. Would you be open to meeting and discussing the possibility?

Eva stared at the screen, her pulse thudding in her ears.

Her first reaction wasn't excitement. It was fear.

Worship Director.

The title felt heavy, almost too big for her shoulders. Memories from years ago came rushing back —late nights of rehearsals, leadership meetings, the constant pressure to get everything right. And beneath it all, the gnawing insecurity: What if I fail again?

She pushed away from the desk, pacing the length of her apartment.

The voice of fear was loud: This is too much. Too risky. If you step into this and fall, it'll be worse than before.

But there was another voice—quiet, steady. The same voice that had whispered to her in the wilderness: I never let go of you.

That evening, Eva sat cross-legged on the floor with her Bible open. She had lit a single candle, letting the soft glow fill the dim room.

Her journal lay beside her, pen poised. She bowed her head and began to write:

Lord, You know my heart. You know my history.
I'm afraid.
I don't want to take a step You haven't asked me to take.
But I also don't want to hide anymore.
Use me, but guide me.
Show me if this is where You want me to stand.
I'm counting on You—not my talent, not my strength. Just You.

The next morning, she took a deep breath and replied to Pastor James.

Yes, I'd like to meet and talk about it. And I'd like to pray with you about it, too.

When she hit "send," she felt something unexpected. Not the crushing weight of responsibility—at least not yet—but a strange lightness.

As if saying yes wasn't about being ready. It was about being willing.

Chapter 23 – With Your Grace

The idea came to her during an early morning prayer walk. The streets were quiet, the first light spilling between the trees, and Eva felt a phrase whisper into her spirit:

Mercy Moves.

She paused mid-step, letting the words settle. They carried a rhythm, almost like a heartbeat.

That week, Eva pitched the concept to Pastor James and the church leadership: a monthly worship night—not a polished production, but a safe space for raw, Spirit-led worship. No programs, no countdown timers, no rigid setlists. Just music, prayer, and the freedom for God's mercy to move however He wanted.

"We'll call it Mercy Moves," she said, her hands open like she was holding something precious. "I don't want it to be about performing. I want it to be about healing—both for the church and for anyone in the community who walks in."

They prayed over it together. By the end of the meeting, it was approved.

The First Mercy Moves Night

It rained that Friday evening, the steady drizzle turning the streets into mirrors of light. Eva arrived early, barefoot on the sanctuary stage, tuning her guitar in the soft hum of anticipation.

One by one, people trickled in—some from the congregation, some from local shelters, a few she recognized from coffee shops and street corners. A group of teens claimed the back row. An older woman in a knitted shawl sat front and center, eyes closed as if already in prayer.

When the lights dimmed, Eva stepped to the mic. Her heart raced, but her voice was steady.

"Tonight isn't about a show," she began. "It's about meeting with God. Whatever you came in carrying, you can set it down here. Let His mercy move in your life."

The first chords rang out—gentle, reverent. The sound filled the room like a warm tide, drawing people in.

They sang old hymns and new choruses, weaving them together as if they had always belonged side by side. Between songs, Eva spoke Scripture over the room:

"Let us then approach God's throne of grace with confidence, so that we may receive mercy and find grace to help us in our time of need." – Hebrews 4:16

Midway through the night, she felt led to pause.

"Some of you came here tonight feeling like you're too far gone," she said, scanning the faces in the dim light. "But mercy moves toward you. Always."

People wept openly. Hands lifted—not in performance, but in surrender.

At one point, Talia slipped quietly into the back. Eva's eyes caught hers, and without a word, they both smiled through tears.

By the end of the night, the altar was lined with people praying—some alone, some with friends, others with complete strangers. The sound of voices praying and soft music blended into something almost tangible, a presence that seemed to linger even as the room emptied.

When Eva finally left, the rain had stopped. The air smelled fresh, like everything had been washed clean.

She whispered into the night, "With Your grace, Lord... I'll make it through."

And for the first time, she wasn't just saying it for herself. She was saying it for all of them.

Chapter 24 – Love Me, Use Me

The prison gates clanged shut behind her, the sound echoing in her bones.

Eva had never been inside a correctional facility before, and everything about it felt heavy—the dim corridors, the stale air, the uniformed guards speaking in clipped tones. She clutched her guitar case as if it were a shield, breathing a prayer with each step.

Lord… this is Your territory before it's theirs. Go before me.

A volunteer from the chaplain's ministry led her into a small multipurpose room. Rows of folding chairs faced a modest podium. There was no stage, no lighting—just a space. A space where walls didn't matter.

The women filed in slowly, wearing identical beige uniforms. Some avoided eye contact, some smiled shyly, and others stared openly, their expressions unreadable.

Eva set her guitar down and introduced herself.

"I'm not here because I've got it all together," she began, her voice steady but warm. "I'm here because I know what it's like to feel unworthy. I know what it's like to believe your story is over."

She told them her story.

The scandal. The shame. The nights she wanted to disappear.

And then—how God met her in the dark, how He whispered that her worth wasn't destroyed by her mistakes. How He called her to stand again, not because she was strong, but because He was.

Her eyes roamed the room as she spoke, and she saw it—recognition. Not pity, not polite interest. Recognition.

She strummed her guitar and began to sing softly. It wasn't a performance—it was a confession set to melody.

Here's where I stand
Here's who I am
Love me, use me, lead me too
And I'll make it through.

A few women closed their eyes. One quietly mouthed the words.

When the song ended, silence settled heavy in the air. Then, a hand in the third row lifted.

It belonged to a young woman with cropped hair and eyes that had seen too much too soon. She stood, voice trembling but clear:

"You said, 'I'm counting on You.'"

Eva nodded, unsure if the woman was repeating it back as a question or a declaration.

The inmate's lips trembled, but she smiled. "I'm saying it now too. I'm counting on Him."

The words landed like a stone in Eva's chest—weighty, undeniable. She felt tears sting her eyes, but she didn't try to stop them.

"Then we're counting on Him together," Eva said softly. "And that means we're already stronger than we were yesterday."

When she left the prison that afternoon, the gates clanged shut again—but this time, the sound didn't feel like an ending. It felt like a bell ringing out over new ground being claimed.

She whispered into the cool air, "Love me, use me, lead me too… and I'll make it through."

And she knew—she wasn't the only one saying it anymore.

Chapter 25 – Lead Me Too

It started with three women in the church café after Sunday service.

Eva had been sipping tea, chatting casually, when one of them leaned forward and asked, "Would you ever mentor young worship leaders? We… could use guidance."

The question caught her off guard. She had just begun to feel stable again in her own calling. The thought of leading others—of shaping them—felt equal parts thrilling and intimidating.

But the answer came quickly, deep in her spirit: Yes.

The Birth of Stand

Two weeks later, she launched a discipleship circle. They named it Stand, after her song. The name carried weight—it wasn't about standing perfectly; it was about standing at all, even with trembling knees.

They met every Thursday night in the small side chapel. No stage, no microphones—just chairs in a circle, guitars leaning against the walls, and Bibles open on laps.

Eva structured the evenings around three rhythms:

Worship – raw, unplugged, and unpolished.

The Word – scripture study tied to worship themes.

Witness – personal testimonies about God's work that week.

One evening, the door opened halfway through worship. A girl slipped in—late teens, hood pulled low over her face, hands shoved deep into the pockets of a worn denim jacket.

She sat in the back, silent, eyes fixed on the floor.

Eva kept singing but couldn't shake the feeling that this girl's presence mattered.

The Mirror

Her name was Kayla.

She had a raspy laugh, a fierce independence, and—Eva noticed quickly—a quiet ache she tried to hide under sarcasm. She rarely made eye contact when she spoke, and she never volunteered to sing.

But when Eva caught her humming along one night, something in her chest stirred.

Kayla reminded her of herself at eighteen—passionate but guarded, full of potential but terrified of being seen.

One evening after the others had left, Eva found her still sitting in the circle, strumming softly on a guitar she'd borrowed.

"You're good," Eva said, leaning on the back of a chair.

Kayla shrugged. "I'm not like you."

Eva smiled. "Good. God didn't make you to be me. He made you to be… well, you."

Kayla finally looked up, something flickering in her eyes—a mix of hope and disbelief.

Passing the Torch

Over the next few weeks, Eva poured into Kayla more intentionally—sharing stories of her own mistakes, her lost years, and the God who had never let go.

One night, during closing prayer, Kayla's voice cracked as she whispered, "Lord, I don't know what You're doing with me… but lead me too."

The words echoed in Eva's heart long after the meeting ended.

This was why she was here—not just to lead songs, but to lead lives into the arms of the One who had carried her all this way.

Chapter 26 – And I'll Make It Through

The late afternoon sun slanted through the windows of the church café, turning the air to gold. Eva was gathering her things after a Stand meeting when she heard the door open.

She didn't look up at first—until she heard the voice.

"Hey, stranger."

Her head snapped up, and there she was. Talia.

Gone was the pale, hollow-cheeked woman Eva had hugged goodbye at the shelter months ago. In her place stood someone radiant—eyes bright, skin warm with color, hair brushed and pulled back neatly.

She wore a simple blue blouse, but it wasn't the clothes that caught Eva's attention. It was the posture. Straight. Confident. Whole.

The Embrace

Eva dropped her bag and crossed the room in three strides. They collided in an embrace that felt like it stitched two stories together—each thread strengthened by surrender.

"I'm sober," Talia whispered against her shoulder, her voice trembling. "Eight months now."

Tears pricked Eva's eyes. "You look… amazing."

Talia laughed softly. "I feel amazing. But more than that… I feel free."

Testimonies in Tandem

They sat down with two mugs of tea, and Talia told her everything.

Rehab hadn't been easy—there were nights she wanted to leave, mornings she didn't think she'd make it through. But she'd clung to prayer, to the scraps of scripture Eva had spoken to her in the shelter's quiet kitchen.

"I remembered what you said," Talia told her. "'Surrender isn't giving up—it's giving in to the One who can carry you.' I finally believed it."

Eva smiled through tears. "You didn't just make it through. You're a living, breathing testimony."

Talia reached across the table, squeezing Eva's hand. "So are you."

The Song Shared

Later that evening, Eva invited Talia to stay for worship practice. She hesitated, then nodded.

When Eva began to sing Here's Where I Stand, she glanced at Talia mid-verse. To her surprise, Talia's lips were moving—singing every word.

Here's where I stand
Here's who I am
Love me, use me, lead me too
And I'll make it through.

The harmony between them wasn't perfect, but it was Spirit-born. Two women—once broken in different ways—now singing the same declaration, woven together in God's redemptive melody.

When the song ended, neither spoke. They didn't have to.

In that moment, Eva knew: this wasn't just her story anymore. It was theirs—and it was still being written.

Chapter 27 – Jesus, I'm Counting on You

The first comment landed like a pebble tossed at a window—sharp enough to make her flinch, small enough to ignore.

Under a short video clip of Here's Where I Stand from the city-wide worship night, someone wrote:

"Funny how people fall from grace and then reinvent themselves when the attention dries up."

Eva read it once, then set down her phone. She'd promised herself she would not go spelunking in the internet's darkest caves. Still, curiosity tugged. She picked the phone up again. Where one pebble falls, others tend to follow.

They did.

"Is this the same Eva Hart from [old church]? Yikes."

"Worship isn't a comeback tour."

"Disqualified leaders should sit down, not get a single."

Her fingers went cold. The room seemed to tilt a few degrees.

She stood, walked to the kitchen sink, and let the faucet run until the water was ice. She cupped her hands and splashed her face. The shock steadied her breathing.

On the counter lay Talia's recent note—creased and smudged from rereading:

Eight months sober. Free. Keep going. Don't stop.

Eva pressed her palms to the counter, eyes closed.

"Jesus," she whispered, "I'm counting on You."

She said it again, a little louder, until it wasn't just air—it was anchor.

At Grace Haven the next morning, the kitchen smelled like cinnamon and coffee. Marlene slid a tray of muffins onto the counter and watched Eva over the rims of her glasses.

"You look like you slept with your phone under your pillow and your enemies in your feed," she said, not unkindly.

Eva gave a rueful huff. "Something like that."

"Do I need to hide your Wi-Fi or your pride?" Marlene asked, mouth quirking.

"Maybe both."

Marlene leaned an elbow on the counter. "You have three choices when folks throw stones online. One: throw them back—satisfying for five minutes, then you feel slimy. Two: pretend the bruises don't hurt—then you rot from the inside out. Three: stand where you are, tell the truth in love, and let Jesus be your soft armor."

"Soft armor?"

"Yeah." She slid over a muffin. "Love's not a wall. It's a cushion. Absorbs impact, doesn't harden your heart."

Eva broke the muffin in half, steam lifting like a prayer. "Soft armor," she repeated. "Okay."

By lunchtime, the posts had multiplied—most were encouragement and testimonies from those who'd been moved by the song. But the sharp ones glinted through the kind ones like broken shell in sand. A few were theological critiques dressed up as concern; others were plain old gossip.

Her phone buzzed. Nate.

Saw the comments. You don't have to answer any of them. But if you do—answer like you sing. True. Clear. No cheap notes.

She stared at the message until a strategy surfaced—not public debate, not silence born of fear. Witness.

She opened her notes app and drafted a post—not a clapback, not a dissertation. A confession and a boundary.

To anyone who's wondering: Yes, I've failed. Yes, I've repented. Yes, I've been under counsel and accountability. God has healed what I broke and what was broken in me. I'm not back to prove anything. I'm here to worship and to serve.

If my story hurts you because of what you've experienced in church, I'm sorry. I can't undo the past, but I can listen and love you now.

If you believe I shouldn't sing, I understand you may feel that way. I won't argue. I'm trusting Jesus to lead me and my leaders to guide me.

If you're struggling with shame, I'm praying for you by name where I can, and by category where I can't. Jesus is near to the brokenhearted. I know because He found me when I was sure I'd disqualified myself.

I'll be in the comments for an hour to pray and point to resources. After that, I'm logging off to be present with the people I'm called to in person. Grace and peace. — Eva

She read it twice, sent it to Pastor Miriam and Nate, waited for their green lights, then posted.

Within minutes, replies stacked up—some softening, some still sharp. She kept her hour, like she had promised. No arguments. No defensiveness. She wrote simple prayers. She DM'd three resources for trauma-informed counseling. She sent a private apology to a woman whose church experience had left wounds that bled when she saw microphones in the hands of imperfect people.

At minute fifty-eight, a new comment appeared from an account with a gray silhouette.

"I was there when everything blew up. I said cruel things. I'm not ready to say I was wrong about all of it… but I was wrong about how I handled it. I don't know what to do with that."

Eva stared at the blinking cursor. She could feel the old ache rise—the reflex to defend, to present Exhibit A and Witness B and the receipts she never posted.

She typed:

Thank you for saying this. That takes courage. If all you can do today is acknowledge the wound—your own and others'—that's a beginning. I'm praying for you. Truly.

She hit send. And then—because she'd promised—she logged off.

She set the phone face-down. The silence that followed wasn't empty.

It was clean.

That evening was Mercy Moves. The sky bruised purple as the sanctuary filled—familiar faces, new ones, a couple of teens still in school hoodies, an older man steadying his wife as they found a seat. Talia arrived early and hugged Eva long and fierce, then took a spot near the front.

Eva tuned her guitar, then looked up. Kayla hovered at the side aisle, hair tucked into a beanie, fingers worrying a pick.

"You ready?" Eva asked.

Kayla lifted a shoulder. "Ready as I'll ever be."

"Good." Eva smiled. "That's usually when the Holy Spirit has the most room."

They began with an old hymn. Voices rose like they'd been waiting all day to exhale. After two songs, Eva spoke—no notes, just what burned in her bones.

"There's been noise this week," she said, hand light on the mic. "About who gets to sing, who's worthy to serve. I want you to hear me: none of us stand here because we're stainless. We stand because Jesus keeps standing us up."

A low murmur of assent swelled, then stilled.

"If the chatter has made you want to hide," she went on, "come closer, not farther. Mercy still moves."

She nodded to Kayla. The girl stepped forward, shoulders high, chin set. Her fingers found a progression—tentative first, then steady. She sang a verse Eva had never heard, words Kayla had written in her bedroom, words that trembled with first-faith:

You don't leave at the rumor /
You don't flinch at the scar /
You hold me where I'm human /
You say I'm still Your art.

The room went very still. By the chorus, people were singing with her, though they didn't know the melody. Love will make a choir out of strangers.

When the song ended, Kayla's eyes were wet. She looked at Eva as if to ask, Was that okay?

Eva nodded once, slow and full. More than okay.

They moved into Here's Where I Stand. Mid-bridge, voices swelled:

I'm counting… oh, I'm counting… I'm counting on You…

Eva heard it then—one voice louder than the rest. Talia's. Not polished. Not shy. Free.

They closed with silence. No flourish. No tag. Just the quiet that follows when heaven has pressed close.

Afterward, as people drifted toward the exits, a woman in a denim jacket approached, hesitation written in the set of her mouth.

"I'm not here to fight," she said before Eva could speak. "I wrote something sharp about you online." She swallowed. "Then I came tonight to confirm I was right. I didn't get what I came for."

"What did you get?" Eva asked gently.

The woman looked down. "Convicted. I'm sorry."

"I forgive you," Eva said, and meant it. "Will you let me pray for you?"

The woman nodded. They prayed. No fireworks. No falling. Just two people standing under the same mercy.

Back home, the quiet of the apartment felt different—like a held note finally allowed to resolve. Eva made tea and sat on the floor beside the coffee table, Bible open to Psalm 27. Her eyes found the words she needed:

"The Lord is my light and my salvation—whom shall I fear? …Though an army besiege me, my heart will not fear; though war break out against me, even then I will be confident."

She smiled at the ancient audacity of it. Then she prayed out loud, voice steady:

"Jesus, I'm counting on You. Not on public approval. Not on spotless history. On You. Teach me to respond with love and to rest with boundaries. Guard my heart from bitterness, my mouth from pride, my mind from rehearsing old court cases. And for every person who hurled a stone today—bless them. Heal what makes them throw. Heal what made me once throw, too."

Her phone buzzed on the table. She let it buzz. Prayer first. Presence first.

When she finally flipped it over, there was a single new text—from an unsaved number.

This is the girl from the comments—the one who said she was there when it blew up. Thank you for how you answered me. I'm not brave enough to apologize publicly yet. But I'm brave enough to ask if we can talk privately sometime. If not, I understand.

Eva stared at the message, then typed back slowly:

Thank you for reaching out. We can talk. No pressure, no performance. Just two people who need Jesus. Here's a time that works…

She hit send, then set the phone down again.

Outside, rain started—soft, steady, like a benediction tapping the glass. Eva leaned her head back against the couch and closed her eyes.

She thought of the girl in the denim jacket. Of Kayla singing. Of Talia's voice ringing clear. Of Marlene's "soft armor." Of Pastor Miriam's steadying presence. Of Nate's texts. Of a Savior who never flinched at the rumor, who never loosened His grip on her hand.

"Jesus," she whispered into the rain-soaked quiet, "I'm still counting on You."

And her heart answered, unshaken:

Here's where I stand.

Chapter 28 – In You I See

The idea began as a whisper in the quiet after prayer—four simple words looping in Eva's spirit like a refrain: In You I see.

At first, she thought it was just the title of a song. But as she sat at her small desk, guitar propped against her leg and journal open to a fresh page, the words kept returning. Not just as a hook. As a statement. A map.

In You I see… grace.
In You I see… identity.
In You I see… courage.
In You I see… me.

The Writing Room

Her apartment transformed into what looked like a creative storm zone—papers strewn across the coffee table, sticky notes climbing the walls like ivy. Lyrics scribbled in pencil and circled in red ink. Verses scratched out, rewritten, then circled again.

She started with the beginning of her journey. The song was raw, minor chords bending under the weight of confession. She called it Here in the Dark. The first verse was nothing but truth:

I hid in shadows, afraid of Your light /
But You saw through the night…

The melody ached, but it didn't stay there. By the second chorus, hope threaded through the lines.

From there, she moved to the songs that marked her turning points. You Took My Shame—written in one sitting—was part ballad, part anthem. She layered it with soft piano and strings, imagining it played in a quiet sanctuary at midnight.

For My Soul's Not Dying, she wanted energy. She called Nate to help with a driving rhythm and let the drums carry the testimony. It wasn't just worship—it was victory in sound.

Writing with Others

One afternoon, Kayla stopped by with her guitar. "You're in album mode," she said, glancing at the clutter. "Mind if I throw in some chords?"

Eva grinned. "Only if you're ready to write the bridge that will make people ugly cry."

Kayla laughed, but within ten minutes, they were sitting cross-legged on the floor, piecing together a bridge for Stand Tall:

Even when the shadows chase me,
Even when the night won't break,
I will lift my hands to heaven,
You're the Light that will not fade.

By the time they finished, Kayla's eyes shimmered. "That's the one people will shout before they even know the words."

The Studio

Recording began in a modest home studio run by a friend from the label. It smelled faintly of coffee and cedar from the acoustic panels.

Standing behind the mic, Eva closed her eyes. "Jesus," she whispered, "I'm not here to sound perfect. I'm here to sound honest."

She sang the opening track with the lights dimmed low, imagining she was back in her apartment on that first night, journal in hand. The sound engineer didn't stop her until the last note faded.

"That," he said softly, "is why this album will matter."

The Tracklist

By the end of the month, twelve songs told her story like a musical memoir:

Here in the Dark – Confession and surrender.

I Come Before You – A simple piano-led prayer.

You Took My Shame – The heart of redemption.

So Much to Give – Serving out of brokenness.

Lord, Please Hear Me – A cry for guidance.

Who I Am – Owning her identity in Christ.

My Soul's Not Dying – Joy breaking through.

In You I'm Stronger – Public worship after years of silence.

Don't Let Go of My Hand – Trust in the middle of fear.

I Walk by Faith – Moving forward without answers.

Stand Tall – Courage to live counted.

In You I See – The title track; an intimate, Spirit-filled declaration.

The Title Track

The last song she recorded was the one the whole project had been pointing to—In You I See. It was slower than she expected, almost a lullaby. The verses painted snapshots of her journey, each ending with the refrain: In You I see… me.

During the final chorus, she asked the engineer to let the mic pick up the sound of her guitar strings squeaking under her fingers, her voice cracking on the highest note. "Keep it in," she said when he offered to re-record. "That's the sound of a real person worshiping, not performing."

When the take was done, she didn't move for a moment. She just let the stillness sit—like the Spirit was sealing the song in her bones.

The Listening Night

A week later, she invited a handful of friends, mentors, and the women from Grace Haven to her apartment. They sat on mismatched chairs and throw pillows while the album played from beginning to end.

Talia sat cross-legged by the window, eyes closed, mouthing the words she already knew. Kayla leaned forward during Stand Tall, hands clasped tight. Pastor Miriam wiped a tear during You Took My Shame.

When the final note of In You I See faded, no one clapped. Not because they didn't want to—but because the moment was holy.

Finally, Talia spoke. "This isn't just your album, Eva. It's ours. You put our prayers in music."

Eva swallowed hard. "Then it's exactly what it was meant to be."

That night, before she went to bed, Eva opened her journal. On the first blank page, she wrote:

Lord, this is my offering. Every chord, every lyric, every crack in my voice—it's all Yours. May these songs find the ones hiding in the dark and show them who they are in You.

She closed the journal, turned off the light, and slept in peace. The kind that only comes when your story, scars and all, has been surrendered back to the Author who wrote it.

Chapter 29 – Here's Where I Stand (Reprise)

The sanctuary smelled faintly of polished wood and candle wax—exactly as it had one year ago.

Back then, Eva had sat in the back pew, trembling, avoiding eye contact, unsure if she belonged. That night, she had walked forward only because her legs seemed to move without permission, collapsing at the altar in a broken plea: God, if You can still use me, I'm here.

Now, she stood in the same place, hands wrapped around the microphone, heart steady.

She hadn't planned for it to fall on the exact date. The worship night was scheduled weeks earlier, and she didn't notice until Pastor Miriam mentioned it: "You know tonight is the anniversary of your altar prayer."

The knowledge sent a shiver down her spine, not of fear, but awe. It wasn't coincidence—it was appointment.

The room filled quickly. Old friends, shelter volunteers, young women from her Stand discipleship circle, even Talia, glowing as always.

As the set began, Eva sang the opening songs with energy, but her heart knew where it was headed. By the time the final chord of the third song faded, she set her guitar down.

She took a step forward and glanced down at the worn spot in the carpet—the spot.

"A year ago," she began, her voice carrying easily in the hushed room, "I stood right here with nothing left to offer God but a mess. My shame told me I was done. My fear told me to run. But His voice…" She paused, swallowing. "…His voice told me, 'Stand.'"

She looked out across the congregation, and this time, she didn't see judgment. She saw faces softened by the same grace that had found her.

"I'm here to tell you tonight—He doesn't waste anything. Not the tears, not the waiting, not the wilderness. Every piece of your story can be redeemed."

She nodded to Nate at the piano. The intro to Here's Where I Stand filled the room, gentle but resolute.

Her voice was soft at first—so soft you could hear her breath between lines.

Here's where I stand

Here's who I am

Love me, use me, lead me too…

The second verse swelled, the band joining in. Strings hummed from the back of the stage.

By the bridge, she stepped back from the mic, lifting her face toward the rafters.

Jesus, Jesus, I'm counting on You…

It was no longer just her voice—others in the room began singing, some with hands raised, some with tears falling. The sound layered, rose, and filled every corner like light breaking through stained glass.

When the final chorus came, Eva's voice didn't tremble. It soared. She sang with the same surrender she had whispered in the dark a year ago—but now it was drenched in confidence.

And I'll make it through…

The last note hung in the air before melting into silence. For a heartbeat, no one moved. Then the applause came—not the polite kind, but the kind that erupted from somewhere deeper than hands.

Eva set the mic down and knelt—not in desperation this time, but in worship.

"Thank You," she whispered, tears slipping down her cheeks. "You kept me. You carried me. And here I stand."

The music faded, but the moment stayed—holy, unhurried. She didn't need anything else. This was enough.

Chapter 30 – This Is Who I Am

The conference hall was a sea of faces—women from every stage of life. Some came in business suits, some in T-shirts and sneakers, others pushing strollers down the aisles. The air buzzed with expectancy, a hum that seemed to rise as the worship band played its final song before introducing her.

Eva waited in the wings, one hand on her notes, the other on the silver cross around her neck. Her heart wasn't pounding from fear this time—it beat with purpose.

Six months earlier, she'd been invited to speak at the National Women of Faith Conference. The email had almost felt like a mistake. Me? But the Lord had been clear: "Say yes."

Now, here she was—about to tell her story, not as someone still crawling from the pit, but as a woman standing in the light.

When her name was called, Eva stepped into the bright glow of the stage lights. Applause rose, but she didn't let it distract her. She scanned the room and found what she was looking for—not the size of the crowd, but the individuals. The woman in the third row clutching a tissue. The teenager leaning forward on the edge of her seat. The grandmother nodding with closed eyes.

She began softly. "One year ago, I was in hiding. Not in a cave or in another city—right here in my own life. I had failed. I had been betrayed. I believed the lie that my calling had an expiration date."

She paused, letting the silence settle.

"But God doesn't use us despite our past. He uses us through it."

The words seemed to ripple across the crowd. A few women murmured "Amen."

She told them about the scandal, the shame, and the nights she cried into her journal. She spoke of the altar, the worship nights, the moments she nearly quit. She didn't skip the ugly parts—she knew those were the very places where God's glory shone the brightest.

Then she shared the turning points: the women's shelter, Talia's friendship, the return to worship, the album In You I See.

Eva stepped closer to the edge of the stage. "You may think your story disqualifies you. You may think your scars are too visible, your mistakes too many. But I'm here as living proof—your story is the very thing God will use to break chains for someone else."

Her voice strengthened. "So stand. Not because you've earned it. Not because you've figured it all out. But because the One who called you hasn't changed His mind about you."

One by one, women rose to their feet—not in applause, but in a quiet, unified movement. Some lifted their hands. Others covered their faces with them. A few stepped into the aisles to kneel and pray.

The band began to play softly, the melody of Here's Where I Stand. Eva joined them—not as a performer, but as a worshiper. The room sang with her, voices weaving together until it felt like heaven itself leaned close to listen.

When it was over, Eva returned to the podium for one final sentence. "This is who I am—a daughter of the King, redeemed and restored. And this is who you are, too."

The applause came, but Eva only smiled. The real victory wasn't in the clapping. It was in the women who would walk out of that room knowing they were not disqualified, not forgotten, and never alone.

Chapter 31 – I Am Yours

The lake was still that morning—like a pane of glass reflecting the soft blush of sunrise. Mist hovered over the water, curling upward in delicate ribbons.

Eva stood barefoot at the shoreline, the hem of her white dress brushing the damp sand. Her hands were steady, but her heart thudded with an almost reverent anticipation.

A small crowd had formed along the edge of the lake—friends from the women's shelter, members of Stand, Eva's church family, and even some of the women who had written letters to her after her album release.

And in the center of them all, walking toward her, was Talia.

She wore simple jeans rolled to her knees and a plain T-shirt, but her face… it glowed. Not just with the joy of the moment, but with the evidence of months of hard-fought freedom.

They met halfway, embracing briefly before stepping into the water together. The cold bit at Eva's legs, but she didn't mind.

"Talia," she said softly, so only the two of them could hear, "are you ready to declare your life belongs to Jesus?"

Talia nodded, tears already welling. "I've been ready since the day He set me free."

Eva took a deep breath, her voice carrying over the gentle lapping of the water.

"Today we witness the outward sign of an inward transformation. Talia stands before us as a daughter of the King, forgiven, restored, and made new."

She looked into Talia's eyes. "Who do you belong to?"

Talia's voice broke as she answered, "I am His. I am Yours, Lord."

Eva smiled, her own tears blurring the sunrise. "Then it's my honor to baptize you in the name of the Father, the Son, and the Holy Spirit."

She lowered Talia gently beneath the surface. For a heartbeat, everything was still—the water rippling around them, the sunlight breaking through the mist.

When Talia rose, gasping and laughing, the crowd erupted into cheers. Water streamed down her face, mixing with tears. She lifted her arms high, a victorious shout leaving her lips: "I am Yours!"

As they walked back to the shore, Eva felt a holy weight settle in her spirit. A year ago, she had been the one barely able to stand, clinging to the hope that God wasn't finished with her. Now, she was standing in the water, helping someone else declare the same truth she had once struggled to believe.

Healing wasn't just hers anymore—it was multiplied, shared, and still unfolding.

And as the morning sun climbed higher, Eva knew this was only the beginning.

Chapter 32 – Here's Who We Are

The church sanctuary pulsed with anticipation. Rows of chairs had been pulled closer to the stage for the Mercy Moves finale, but tonight was different—Eva's Stand discipleship circle was taking the lead.

Every woman on the stage had her own story—rescued from addiction, healed from abuse, restored from doubt. And every one of them had been mentored by Eva in some way.

The Song's Birth

It had started as a casual songwriting exercise in Eva's living room—Bibles open, coffee mugs half-empty. But the Holy Spirit moved, and within two hours, they had a melody, a refrain, and a title: We Are Yours.

The lyrics were simple but powerful—woven from Scripture, testimony, and prayer.

The Stage Moment

Tonight, the lights dimmed except for a warm spotlight bathing the group. Guitars hummed, a piano chord rang out, and the first voice began—soft, almost trembling.

Once we were broken, afraid and unknown
Now we are chosen, we're never alone

Another voice joined in, harmonizing as the drumbeat began to build.

We are Yours, we are Yours
Redeemed by Your mercy, held by Your love

Eva stood off to the side, not leading, but singing with them. Her heart swelled as each woman stepped forward to sing a line that had been born from her own story.

The Congregation Joins

By the second chorus, the sanctuary was on its feet. Hands rose. Some swayed, some wept openly. The refrain repeated, the voices of the congregation blending into a single, soaring declaration:

We are Yours, we are Yours
Jesus forever, we are Yours

The Declaration

As the music slowed, one of the younger members—Lena, just nineteen—took the mic. "This song is more than words. It's our testimony. We stand here not as perfect women, but as women made new. And we're here to tell you—there's room for you in this 'we.'"

The room was silent except for the sniffles and soft "Amens."

The final chord lingered in the air, then faded into an unplanned moment of prayer. People came forward to the altar—some for the first time, some returning after years away.

Eva closed her eyes, letting the sound of voices and the smell of anointing oil wash over her. This wasn't just a song. It was a banner. A declaration.

This was who they were.
And this was who they would always be.

Chapter 33 – Grace Carried Me

The rain tapped lightly against Eva's window, a gentle rhythm that seemed to sync with her thoughts. Her desk was cluttered with letters—some handwritten in neat cursive, others on folded notebook paper, still others typed and printed, the ink slightly smudged.

She traced her fingers over the top one. To the woman who reminded me I'm not too far gone…

Eva's Flashback

She remembered the night she'd first walked into the women's shelter, serving coffee and hiding behind her pain. Back then, she had no idea that grace could still move through her, let alone transform her.

Her mind flickered to that lakeside morning when she baptized Talia—the way the water reflected the sunrise, the way the crowd's cheer seemed to echo in heaven.

She whispered now, as if to the Lord Himself: "You carried me the whole time, didn't You?"

Talia's Letter

Eva unfolded a letter from Talia, written in her loopy handwriting.

Eva,
I don't just thank you for mentoring me. I thank you for showing me that grace is more than a second chance—it's a constant presence. I've enrolled in Bible college. I want to help women like you helped me. Grace carried me here.

Eva smiled, tears blurring the ink.

Lena's Flashback

Her mind shifted to Lena, the nineteen-year-old who had sung on stage during We Are Yours. She'd walked into Stand unsure of her voice—both musically and spiritually. Now, she was leading worship at her own church, sending Eva a text last week: We used "We Are Yours" again tonight. People were crying in the aisles.

Eva closed her eyes and saw it clearly: grace flowing like a current, from one heart to another.

The Women's Voices

She picked up more letters—each one a thread.

I was ready to give up, but you reminded me of the God who still calls me.
I've learned that my scars are not shame—they're stories.
Your honesty freed me to be honest with God for the first time.

Each testimony was different, but all pointed to the same truth: grace was the bridge that had carried them.

Eva's Prayer

Eva leaned back, the letters spread before her like a mosaic. She prayed aloud, her voice soft but steady.

"Lord, thank You for every step, every stumble, every rescue. Thank You that we never walk alone. Grace carried me, and it will carry them, too."

The Final Scene

That Sunday, Eva stood at the front of the church—not with a sermon, but with an open invitation. She held up a single piece of paper with the words Grace Carried Me written across it.

"This is my story," she said, her voice carrying across the sanctuary. "But it's also yours. And if you're still in the middle of the storm, hold on—because grace is already on its way."

One by one, people came forward—some to pray, some to worship, some simply to weep in relief.

And as the music swelled, Eva knew this was not the end. It was the continuation of the same thread, weaving through every life, binding them together in the hands of the One who carried them all.

Chapter 35 – I'll Make It Through

The stage lights were warm against her skin, but Eva barely noticed. The sanctuary was filled to the brim—faces from every chapter of her journey. Women from Stand, Talia's family, members of the shelter, her old church family, and strangers who had simply heard the songs and felt something stir.

Tonight wasn't about an album release, a title, or a performance. Tonight was about gratitude. About standing in the very place she had once fallen and declaring—without hesitation—that God's grace had been enough.

The Opening Chords

The first soft strum of the guitar filled the room. Eva closed her eyes and lifted her head slightly. Her hands rose—not in desperation, as they once had, but in assurance. She didn't come tonight as the broken girl begging for a second chance. She came as the daughter of God who had been carried through fire, through shame, through the wilderness, and into the light.

She began to sing.

Here's where I stand
Here's who I am
With You, I'll make it through

The words weren't just lyrics anymore—they were her testimony.

The Congregation Joins

One by one, voices rose from the crowd. First the worship team. Then the front rows. Soon the entire room was singing with her. The sound swelled, a unified chorus that seemed to shake the walls.

Eva opened her eyes and saw people with hands lifted, some with tears streaming down their cheeks, some smiling with the kind of joy that only comes from freedom.

She spotted Talia in the front row, singing with both hands stretched high, eyes closed in pure worship.

The Bridge

The bridge hit, and Eva stepped back from the mic, letting the crowd's voices lead.

I'm counting on You
I'm counting on You
I'm counting on You

The repetition felt like waves crashing over her, each one washing away the last traces of the woman she used to be.

The Final Note

As the song reached its final refrain, Eva's voice blended with hundreds of others:

With You, I'll make it through

The music faded, but the worship didn't. People lingered in the moment, hands still lifted, whispers of prayer and praise filling the air like incense.

Eva lowered her arms, smiling through tears. She had made it through—not by her strength, not by her perfection, but by His grace alone.

And she knew—whatever came next, she'd keep standing.

Epilogue – Standing Together

Five years later, the sanctuary looked different—larger, brighter, with new stained glass casting warm light across the pews. But the spirit of the place felt the same.

Eva stood at the back for a moment, watching as a group of young women tuned guitars and adjusted microphones. Stand had grown from a living room circle into a nationwide network, training and mentoring women in worship and ministry.

Talia was now one of its directors, standing at the front of the stage with the same sparkle in her eyes she'd worn at her baptism. She caught Eva's gaze and smiled, lifting a hand in greeting before returning to her notes.

Eva took her seat in the front row, heart swelling as she saw Lena—now in her mid-twenties—leading the rehearsal for tonight's worship night. This time, the stage was filled with faces Eva didn't recognize, girls she hadn't personally mentored but who had been mentored by those she had poured into.

It was the ripple effect she had prayed for, now in full motion.

When the service began, the first song was one Eva knew by heart: We Are Yours. The lyrics hadn't changed, but the voices were new, layered with fresh testimony.

She closed her eyes as they sang the chorus:

We are Yours, we are Yours
Jesus forever, we are Yours

It struck her—this song had outlived her own leadership of it. That was the point. It was never about her.

Halfway through the night, Talia invited Eva to the stage. "I think it's only right," she said into the mic, "that we honor the one who reminded us to stand."

Eva stepped forward, not to take over, but to kneel. Others followed. The altar filled—not with brokenness alone, but with gratitude, worship, and joy.

In that moment, the generations blended: the women Eva had mentored, the women they had mentored, and those just beginning their journeys.

Final Reflection

Eva lifted her hands, smiling through tears. She wasn't the woman from Here in the Dark anymore. She wasn't even the woman who had sung Here's Where I Stand for the first time.

She was a daughter of God—still learning, still walking by faith, still carried by grace. And she knew the truth in her bones:

As long as they stood together, their stories would never stop pointing to Him.

Author's Note

Author's Note

When I first began writing Here's Where I Stand, I had no idea how much of my own story would pour onto the page. Though Eva is a fictional character, her journey mirrors what so many of us walk through—seasons of shame, seasons of silence, and finally, the tender call of Jesus reminding us: You are still Mine.

This novel is more than a story—it is a prayer. Every chapter reflects the truth that God's grace meets us in the darkest valleys, that surrender is not weakness but freedom, and that our past does not disqualify us from being used by Him. In fact, it is often the very place where His power shines the brightest.

To every reader who feels broken, forgotten, or unworthy—this book is for you. May you see yourself in Eva's trembling steps and in her lifted hands. May you hear the whisper of Jesus reminding you, "Here's where you stand. Here's who you are. You are Mine."

Thank you for walking this journey with me. If even one life is touched, if even one heart remembers they are seen and loved by God, then this story has done what it was meant to do.

With love and faith,
JanayJourney

Reader Reflection & Discussion Guide

Here's Where I Stand isn't just Eva's story—it's an invitation to reflect on your own. Use these prompts as personal journal entries, small group discussion starters, or quiet prayer reflections.

Chapters 1–5: The Cry in the Dark

Have you ever felt spiritually distant, ashamed, or "too far gone"?

What role has shame played in silencing your gifts or calling?

How do you usually cry out to God—in prayer, writing, music, or silence?

Chapters 6–10: The Stirring of Hope

Eva began serving again in small, hidden ways. Where might God be nudging you to quietly serve right now?

What helps you remember that your identity is not in your mistakes but in Christ?

Write a prayer asking God to "hear you" in the place you most need Him.

Chapters 11–15: The Breaking & the Healing

Eva's worship was raw, imperfect, yet powerful. Do you struggle with perfectionism in faith?

How can vulnerability become a strength rather than a weakness in your walk with Jesus?

Recall a season where God allowed you to walk through the "wilderness." What did you learn?

Chapters 16–20: Standing Tall

When has God reminded you of who you are in Him?

Eva faced opportunities but wrestled with fear. What step of faith feels risky to you right now?

Imagine yourself standing on stage, declaring, "Here's where I stand." What would you be saying?

Chapters 21–25: Living Called

What does it mean to be "counted" in God's kingdom?

How can you mentor or support others out of your testimony?

Write a letter to someone younger in the faith—what words of encouragement would you share?

Chapters 26–30: Full Circle Faith

How have you seen God redeem past failures into ministry or testimony?

Eva's final message: "God doesn't use us despite our past. He uses us through it." How does this truth speak to you?

What is your "Here's Where I Stand" declaration today? Write it out as a prayer or affirmation.

Reader Reflection & Prayer Guide

Here's Where I Stand isn't just Eva's story—it's an invitation to reflect on your own. Use these prompts as personal journal entries, small group discussion starters, or quiet prayer reflections.

Chapters 1–5: The Cry in the Dark

Have you ever felt spiritually distant, ashamed, or "too far gone"?

What role has shame played in silencing your gifts or calling?

How do you usually cry out to God—in prayer, writing, music, or silence?

Prayer:
Lord, in my darkest moments, remind me that You are near. Replace my shame with Your mercy, and help me lift my voice to You again.

Chapters 6–10: The Stirring of Hope

Eva began serving again in small, hidden ways. Where might God be nudging you to quietly serve right now?

What helps you remember that your identity is not in your mistakes but in Christ?

Write a prayer asking God to "hear you" in the place you most need Him.

Prayer:

Father, thank You for reminding me that even small steps of service matter. Anchor my identity in You alone, and let me trust that You hear my every prayer.

Chapters 11–15: The Breaking & the Healing

Eva's worship was raw, imperfect, yet powerful. Do you struggle with perfectionism in faith?

How can vulnerability become a strength rather than a weakness in your walk with Jesus?

Recall a season where God allowed you to walk through the "wilderness." What did you learn?

Prayer:
Jesus, thank You for meeting me in my weakness. Teach me to see my brokenness as a place where Your strength shines brightest.

Chapters 16–20: Standing Tall

When has God reminded you of who you are in Him?

Eva faced opportunities but wrestled with fear. What step of faith feels risky to you right now?

Imagine yourself standing on stage, declaring, "Here's where I stand." What would you be saying?

Prayer:
Lord, give me the courage to step into the calling You've placed before me. Help me stand tall in Your truth, not in my own strength.

Chapters 21–25: Living Called

What does it mean to be "counted" in God's kingdom?

How can you mentor or support others out of your testimony?

Write a letter to someone younger in the faith—what words of encouragement would you share?

Prayer:
God, thank You that I am counted and chosen in Your kingdom. Use my story to bless and guide others, so that they may also walk in Your truth.

Chapters 26–30: Full Circle Faith

How have you seen God redeem past failures into ministry or testimony?

Eva's final message: "God doesn't use us despite our past. He uses us through it." How does this truth speak to you?

What is your "Here's Where I Stand" declaration today? Write it out as a prayer or affirmation.

Prayer:
Heavenly Father, thank You for turning ashes into beauty. I stand in Your grace today, declaring that my past is not my prison—it's the place where Your glory is revealed.

About the Author

JanayJourney is a passionate storyteller, devoted mother of three, and a creative force who thrives in the world of imagination. Under her pen name, she weaves gripping tales filled with twists, emotional drama, and unexpected turns—spanning horror, fantasy, supernatural, romance, and faith-based inspiration.

Her novels explore the fragile beauty of love, the resilience of the human spirit, and the messy truth of finding yourself after loss. When she's not crafting page-turning plots or developing unforgettable characters, Janay pours her heart into songwriting, penning soul-stirring lyrics with the same emotions she brings to her fiction.

A lifelong lover of stories, she finds joy and inspiration in reading light novels during quiet moments, often drawing from their charm to fuel her own narratives. Whether it's spine-chilling suspense, heart-fluttering romance, or worlds filled with magic and mystery, JanayJourney writes with passion, purpose, and a deep love for the art of storytelling.

To read more of her work and follow her creative journey, visit her on:
📚 Inkitt, WebNovel, Wattpad, Royal Road, and other platforms.

Also by JanayJourney

✨ ✨ Here's Where I Stand – An inspirational Christian novel of redemption, identity, and surrender to God's plan.

✨ Sophie's Story – A tearjerker of faith, family, and grace in the face of illness and goodbye.

✨ Whitney's Kitchen – A heartfelt, faith-rooted story of motherhood, love, and legacy woven through food, family, and faith.

✨ The True Meaning of a Lover – A sweeping drama of love, resilience, and building legacy through forgiveness and endurance.

✨ Waste of Your Time – An emotional journey of heartbreak, self-discovery, and courage after toxic love.

✨ Echoes of the Abyss – A haunting psychological WebNovel where one man fights through shadows, fear, and fragments of his soul.

✨ Twin Flames – A spiritual romance about two souls destined to find each other across lifetimes, no matter the odds.

✨ Angelika's SUMMER – A steamy, small-town romance of passion, healing, and unexpected love.

✧ Moonshadow – A mystical fantasy of divine lineage, forbidden love, and destiny beneath a cursed moon.

✧ Reborn Vengeance – A powerful tale of betrayal, rebirth, and a girl determined to protect her family with her second chance.

Coming Soon

✿ The Garden of Forgiveness – A deeply moving novel about letting go, blooming again, and the beauty found in surrender.

⚡ Power Line – A riveting historical fiction set in 1970s New York, exploring legacy, survival, and the cost of truth.

🌐 Moonshadow: Bloodline – The anticipated sequel continuing Luna's divine and dangerous journey.

♥ Grace Carried Me – An intimate story of redemption and healing told through letters, worship, and memory.

🌙 The Reckoning Moon – A cinematic sci-fi thriller where survival collides with destiny on a lunar battlefield.

👗 Allure of the Red Dress – A romantic drama set in New Orleans, where love, jazz, and legacy intertwine beneath the glow of Bourbon Street.

Printed in Dunstable, United Kingdom